POIROT SHORT STORIES

KU-208-528

The ABC Murders
The Adventure of the
    Christmas Pudding
After the Funeral
And Then There Were None
Appointment with Death
At Bertram's Hotel
The Big Four
The Body in the Library
By the Pricking of My Thumbs
Cards on the Table
A Caribbean Mystery
Cat Among the Pigeons
The Clocks
Crooked House
Curtain: Poirot's Last Case
Dead Man's Folly
Death Comes as the End
Death in the Clouds
Death on the Nile
Destination Unknown
Dumb Witness
Elephants Can Remember
Endless Night
Evil Under the Sun
Five Little Pigs
4.50 from Paddington
Hallowe'en Party
Hercule Poirot's Christmas
Hickory Dickory Dock
The Hollow
The Hound of Death
The Labours of Hercules
The Listerdale Mystery
Lord Edgware Dies
The Man in the Brown Suit
The Mirror Crack'd from Side
    to Side
Miss Marple's Final Cases
The Moving Finger
Mrs McGinty's Dead
The Murder at the Vicarage
Murder in Mesopotamia
Murder in the Mews
A Murder is Announced
Murder is Easy
The Murder of Roger Ackroyd
Murder on the Links
Murder on the Orient Express

The Mysterious Affair at Styles
The Mysterious Mr Quin
The Mystery of the Blue Train
Nemesis
N or M?
One, Two, Buckle My Shoe
Ordeal by Innocence
The Pale Horse
Parker Pyne Investigates
Partners in Crime
Passenger to Frankfurt
Peril at End House
A Pocket Full of Rye
Poirot Investigates
Poirot's Early Cases
Postern of Fate
Problem at Pollensa Bay
Sad Cypress
The Secret Adversary
The Secret of Chimneys
The Seven Dials Mystery
The Sittaford Mystery
Sleeping Murder
Sparkling Cyanide
Taken at the Flood
They Came to Baghdad
They Do It With Mirrors
Third Girl
The Thirteen Problems
Three-Act Tragedy
Towards Zero
Why Didn't They Ask Evans

*Novels under the Nom de Plume of
'Mary Westmacott'*
Absent in the Spring
The Burden
A Daughter's A Daughter
Giant's Bread
The Rose and the Yew Tree
Unfinished Portrait

*Books under the name of
Agatha Christie Mallowan*
Come Tell me How You Live
Star Over Bethlehem

Autobiography
Agatha Christie: An Autobiography

AGATHA CHRISTIE

POIROT
SHORT STORIES

This edition specially produced in 1996
for Addis Housewares by the Outhouse Marketing
and Design Company in conjunction with
HarperCollins*Publishers*
77–85 Fulham Palace Road,
Hammersmith, London W6 8JB

Adapted from Poirot's Early Cases,
first published by Collins 1974

ISBN 0 583 32622 6

Printed in Great Britain

CONTENTS

THE AFFAIR AT THE VICTORY BALL

Pure chance led my friend Hercule Poirot, formerly chief of the Belgian force, to be connected with the Styles Case. His success brought him notoriety, and he decided to devote himself to the solving of problems in crime. Having been wounded on the Somme and invalided out of the Army, I finally took up my quarters with him in London. Since I have a first-hand knowledge of most of his cases, it has been suggested to me that I select some of the most interesting and place them on record. In doing so, I feel that I cannot do better than begin with that strange tangle which aroused such widespread public interest at the time. I refer to the affair at the Victory Ball.

Although perhaps it is not so fully demonstrative of Poirot's peculiar methods as some of the more obscure cases, its sensational features, the well-known people involved, and the tremendous publicity given it by the Press, make it stand out as a *cause célèbre* and I have long felt that it is only fitting that Poirot's connection with the solution should be given to the world.

It was a fine morning in spring, and we were sitting in Poirot's rooms. My little friend, neat and dapper as ever, his egg-shaped head tilted on one side, was delicately applying a new pomade to his moustache. A certain harmless vanity was a characteristic of Poirot's and fell into line with his general love of order and method. The *Daily Newsmonger*, which I had been reading, had slipped to the floor, and I was deep in a brown study when Poirot's voice recalled me.

'Of what are you thinking so deeply, *mon ami*?'

'To tell you the truth,' I replied, 'I was puzzling over this unaccountable affair at the Victory Ball. The papers are full of it.' I tapped the sheet with my finger as I spoke.

'Yes?'

'The more one reads of it, the more shrouded in mystery the whole thing becomes!' I warmed to my subject. 'Who killed Lord Cronshaw? Was Coco Courtenay's death on the same night a mere coincidence? Was it an accident? Or did she deliberately take an overdose of cocaine?' I stopped, and then added dramatically: 'These are the questions I ask myself.'

Poirot, somewhat to my annoyance, did not play up. He was peering into the glass, and merely murmured: 'Decidedly, this new pomade, it is a marvel for the moustaches!' Catching my eye, however, he added hastily: 'Quite so – and how do you reply to your questions?'

But before I could answer, the door opened, and our landlady announced Inspector Japp.

The Scotland Yard man was an old friend of ours and we greeted him warmly.

'Ah, my good Japp,' cried Poirot, 'and what brings you to see us?'

'Well, Monsieur Poirot,' said Japp, seating himself and nodding to me, 'I'm on a case that strikes me as being very much in your line, and I came along to know whether you'd care to have a finger in the pie?'

Poirot had a good opinion of Japp's abilities, though deploring his lamentable lack of method, but I, for my part, considered that the detective's highest talent lay in the gentle art of seeking favours under the guise of conferring them!

'It's the Victory Ball,' said Japp persuasively. 'Come, now, you'd like to have a hand in that.'

Poirot smiled at me.

'My friend Hastings would, at all events. He was just holding forth on the subject, *n-est-ce pas, mon ami*?'

'Well, sir,' said Japp condescendingly, 'you shall be in it too. I can tell you, it's something of a feather in your cap to have inside knowledge of a case like this. Well, here's to business. You know the main facts of the case, I suppose, Monsieur Poirot?'

'From the papers only – and the imagination of the journalist is sometimes misleading. Recount the whole story to me.'

Japp crossed his legs comfortably and began.

8

'As all the world and his wife knows, on Tuesday last a grand Victory Ball was held. Every twopenny-halfpenny hop calls itself that nowadays, but this was the real thing, held at the Colossus Hall, and all London at it – including your Lord Cronshaw and his party.'

'His *dossier*?' interrupted Poirot. 'I should say his bioscope – no, how do you call it – biograph?'

'Viscount Cronshaw was fifth viscount, twenty-five years of age, rich, unmarried, and very fond of the theatrical world. There were rumours of his being engaged to Miss Courtenay of the Albany Theatre, who was known to her friends as "Coco" and who was, by all accounts, a very fascinating young lady.'

'Good. *Continuez!*'

'Lord Cronshaw's party consisted of six people: he himself, his uncle, the Honourable Eustace Beltane, a pretty American widow, Mrs Mallaby, a young actor, Chris Davidson, his wife, and last but not least, Miss Coco Courtenay. It was a fancy dress ball, as you know, and the Cronshaw party represented the old Italian Comedy – whatever that may be.'

'The *Commedia dell' Arte*,' murmured Poirot. 'I know.'

'Anyway, the costumes were copied from a set of china figures forming part of Eustace Beltane's collection. Lord Cronshaw was Harlequin; Beltane was Punchinello; Mrs Mallaby matched him as Pulcinella; the Davidsons were Pierrot and Pierette; and Miss Courtenay, of course, was Columbine. Now, quite early in the evening it was apparent that there was something wrong. Lord Cronshaw was moody and strange in his manner. When the party met together for supper in a small private room engaged by the host, everyone noticed that he and Miss Courtenay were no longer on speaking terms. She had obviously been crying, and seemed on the verge of hysterics. The meal was an uncomfortable one, and as they all left the supper-room, she turned to Chris Davidson and requested him audibly to take her home, as she was "sick of the ball". The young actor hesitated, glancing at Lord Cronshaw, and finally drew them both back to the supper-room.

'But all his efforts to secure a reconciliation were unavailing,

9

and he accordingly got a taxi and escorted the now weeping Miss Courtenay back to her flat. Although obviously very much upset, she did not confide in him, merely reiterating again and again that she would "make old Cronch sorry for this!" That is the only hint we have that her death might not have been accidental, and it's precious little to go upon. By the time Davidson had quieted her down somewhat, it was too late to return to the Colossus Hall, and Davidson accordingly went straight home to his flat in Chelsea, where his wife arrived shortly afterwards, bearing the news of the terrible tragedy that had occurred after his departure.

'Lord Cronshaw, it seems, became more and more moody as the ball went on. He kept away from his party, and they hardly saw him during the rest of the evening. It was about one-thirty a.m., just before the grand cotillion when everyone was to unmask, that Captain Digby, a brother officer who knew his disguise, noticed him standing in a box gazing down on the scene.

' "Hullo, Cronch!" he called. "Come down and be sociable! What are you moping about up there for like a boiled owl? Come along; there's a good old rag coming on now."

' "Right!" responded Cronshaw. "Wait for me, or I'll never find you in the crowd."

'He turned and left the box as he spoke. Captain Digby, who had Mrs Davidson with him, waited. The minutes passed, but Lord Cronshaw did not appear. Finally Digby grew impatient.

' "Does the fellow think we're going to wait all night for him?" he exclaimed.

'At that moment Mrs Mallaby joined them, and they explained the situation.

' "Say, now," cried the pretty widow vivaciously, "he's like a bear with a sore head tonight. Let's go right away and rout him out."

'The search commenced, but met with no success until it occurred to Mrs Mallaby that he might possibly be found in the room where they had supped an hour earlier. They made their way there. What a sight met their eyes! There was

Harlequin, sure enough, but stretched on the ground with a table-knife in his heart!'

Japp stopped, and Poirot nodded, and said with the relish of the specialist: '*Une belle affaire*! And there was no clue as to the perpetrator of the deed? But how should there be!'

'Well,' continued the inspector, 'you know the rest. The tragedy was a double one. Next day there were headlines in all the papers, and a brief statement to the effect that Miss Courtenay, the popular actress, had been discovered dead in her bed, and that her death was due to an overdose of cocaine. Now, was it accident or suicide? Her maid, who was called upon to give evidence, admitted that Miss Courtenay was a confirmed taker of the drug, and a verdict of accidental death was returned. Nevertheless we can't leave the possibility of suicide out of account. Her death is particularly unfortunate, since it leaves us no clue now to the cause of the quarrel the preceding night. By the way, a small enamel box was found on the dead man. It had *Coco* written across it in diamonds, and was half full of cocaine. It was identified by Miss Courtenay's maid as belonging to her mistress, who nearly always carried it about with her, since it contained her supply of the drug to which she was fast becoming a slave.'

'Was Lord Cronshaw himself addicted to the drug?'

'Very far from it. He held unusually strong views on the subject of dope.'

Poirot nodded thoughtfully.

'But since the box was in his possession, he knew that Miss Courtenay took it. Suggestive, that, is it not, my good Japp?'

'Ah!' said Japp rather vaguely.

I smiled.

'Well,' said Japp, 'that's the case. What do you think of it?'

'You found no clue of any kind that has not been reported?'

'Yes, there was this.' Japp took a small object from his pocket and handed it over to Poirot. It was a small pompon of emerald green silk, with some ragged threads hanging from it, as though it had been wrenched violently away.

'We found it in the dead man's hand, which was tightly clenched over it,' explained the inspector.

11

Poirot handed it back without any comment and asked: 'Had Lord Cronshaw any enemies?'

'None that anyone knows of. He seemed a popular young fellow.'

'Who benefits by his death?'

'His uncle, the Honourable Eustace Beltane, comes into the title and estates. There are one or two suspicious facts against him. Several people declare that they heard a violent altercation going on in the little supper-room, and that Eustace Beltane was one of the disputants. You see, the table-knife being snatched up off the table would fit in with the murder being done in the heat of a quarrel.'

'What does Mr Beltane say about the matter?'

'Declares one of the waiters was the worse for liquor, and that he was giving him a dressing down. Also that it was nearer to one than half past. You see, Captain Digby's evidence fixes the time pretty accurately. Only about ten minutes elapsed between his speaking to Cronshaw and the finding of the body.'

'And in any case I suppose Mr Beltane, as Punchinello, was wearing a hump and a ruffle?'

'I don't know the exact details of the costumes,' said Japp, looking curiously at Poirot. 'And anyway, I don't quite see what that has got to do with it?'

'No?' There was a hint of mockery in Poirot's smile. He continued quietly, his eyes shining with the green light I had learned to recognize so well: 'There was a curtain in this little supper-room, was there not?'

'Yes, but –'

'With a space behind it sufficient to conceal a man?'

'Yes – in fact, there's a small recess, but how you knew about it – you haven't been to the place, have you, Monsieur Poirot?'

'No, my good Japp, I supplied the curtain from my brain. Without it, the drama is not reasonable. And always one must be reasonable. But tell me, did they not send for a doctor?'

'At once, of course. But there was nothing to be done. Death must have been instantaneous.'

Poirot nodded rather impatiently.

'Yes, yes, I understand. This doctor, now, he gave evidence at the inquest?'

'Yes.'

'Did he say nothing of any unusual symptom – was there nothing about the appearance of the body which struck him as being abnormal?'

Japp stared hard at the little man.

'Yes, Monsieur Poirot. I don't know what you're getting at, but he did mention that there was a tension and stiffness about the limbs which he was quite at a loss to account for.'

'Aha!' said Poirot. 'Aha! *Mon Dieu*! Japp, that gives one to think, does it not?'

I saw that it had certainly not given Japp to think.

'If you're thinking of poison, monsieur, who on earth would poison a man first and then stick a knife into him?'

'In truth that would be ridiculous,' agreed Poirot placidly.

'Now is there anything you want to see, monsieur? If you'd like to examine the room where the body was found –'

Poirot waved his hand.

'Not in the least. You have told me the only thing that interests me – Lord Cronshaw's views on the subject of drug taking.'

'Then there's nothing you want to see?'

'Just one thing.'

'What is that?'

'The set of china figures from which the costumes were copied.'

Japp stared.

'Well, you're a funny one!'

'You can manage that for me?'

'Come round to Berkeley Square now if you like. Mr Beltane – or His Lordship, as I should say now – won't object.'

We set off at once in a taxi. The new Lord Cronshaw was not at home, but at Japp's request we were shown into the 'china room', where the gems of the collection were kept. Japp looked round him rather helplessly.

'I don't see how you'll ever find the ones you want, monsieur.'

But Poirot had already drawn a chair in front of the mantelpiece and was hopping up upon it like a nimble robin. Above the mirror, on a small shelf to themselves, stood six china figures. Poirot examined them minutely, making a few comments to us as he did so.

'*Les voilà*! The old Italian Comedy. Three pairs! Harlequin and Columbine, Pierrot and Pierrette – very dainty in white and green – and Punchinello and Pulcinella in mauve and yellow. Very elaborate, the costume of Punchinello – ruffles and frills, a hump, a high hat. Yes, as I thought, very elaborate.'

He replaced the figures carefully, and jumped down.

Japp looked unsatisfied, but as Poirot had clearly no intention of explaining anything, the detective put the best face he could upon the matter. As we were preparing to leave, the master of the house came in, and Japp performed the necessary introductions.

The sixth Viscount Cronshaw was a man of about fifty, suave in manner, with a handsome, dissolute face. Evidently an elderly roué, with the languid manner of a poseur. I took an instant dislike to him. He greeted us graciously enough, declaring he had heard great accounts of Poirot's skill, and placing himself at our disposal in every way.

'The police are doing all they can, I know,' Poirot said.

'But I much fear the mystery of my nephew's death will never be cleared up. The whole thing seems utterly mysterious.'

Poirot was watching him keenly. 'Your nephew had no enemies that you know of?'

'None whatever. I am sure of that.' He paused, and then went on: 'If there are any questions you would like to ask – '

'Only one.' Poirot's voice was serious. 'The costumes – they were reproduced *exactly* from your figurines?'

'To the smallest detail.'

'Thank you, milor'. That is all I wanted to be sure of. I wish you good day.'

'And what next?' inquired Japp as we hurried down the street. 'I've got to report at the Yard, you know.'

'*Bien*! I will not detain you. I have one other little matter to attend to, and then – '

'Yes?'

'The case will be complete.'

'What? You don't mean it! You know who killed Lord Cronshaw?'

'*Parfaitement.*'

'Who was it? Eustace Beltane?'

'Ah, *mon ami*, you know my little weakness! Always I have a desire to keep the threads in my own hands up to the last minute. But have no fear. I will reveal all when the time comes. I want no credit – the affair shall be yours, on the condition that you permit me to play out the *dénouement* my own way.'

'That's fair enough,' said Japp. 'That is, if the *dénouement* ever comes! But I say, you *are* an oyster, aren't you?' Poirot smiled. 'Well, so long. I'm off to the Yard.'

He strode off down the steet, and Poirot hailed a passing taxi.

'Where are we going now?' I asked in lively curiosity.

'To Chelsea to see the Davidsons.'

He gave the address to the driver.

'What do you think of the new Lord Cronshaw?' I asked.

'What says my good friend Hastings?'

'I distrust him instinctively.'

'You think he is the "wicked uncle" of the story-books, eh?'

'Don't you?'

'Me, I think he was most amiable towards us,' said Poirot noncommittally.

'Because he had his reasons!'

Poirot looked at me, shook his head sadly, and murmured something that sounded like: 'No method.'

The Davidsons lived on the third floor of a block of 'mansion' flats. Mr Davidson was out, we were told, but Mrs Davidson was at home. We were ushered into a long, low room with garish Oriental hangings. The air felt close and oppressive, and there was an overpowering fragrance of joss-sticks. Mrs

Davidson came to us almost immediately, a small, fair creature whose fragility would have seemed pathetic and appealing had it not been for the rather shrewd and calculating gleam in her light blue eyes.

Poirot explained our connection with the case, and she shook her head sadly.

'Poor Cronch – and poor Coco too! We were both so fond of her, and her death has been a terrible grief to us. What is it you want to ask me? Must I really go over all that dreadful evening again?'

'Oh, madame, believe me, I would not harass your feelings unnecessarily. Indeed, Inspector Japp has told me all that is needful. I only wish to see the costume you wore at the ball that night.'

The lady looked somewhat surprised, and Poirot continued smoothly: 'You comprehend, madame, that I work on the system of my country. There we always "reconstruct" the crime. It is possible that I may have an actual *représentation*, and if so, you understand, the costumes would be important.'

Mrs Davidson still looked a bit doubtful.

'I've heard of reconstructing a crime, of course,' she said. 'But I didn't know you were so particular about details. But I'll fetch the dress now.'

She left the room and returned almost immediately with a dainty wisp of white satin and green. Poirot took it from her and examined it, handing it back with a bow.

'*Merci, madame*! I see you have had the misfortune to lose one of your green pompons, the one on the shoulder here.'

'Yes, it got torn off at the ball. I picked it up and gave it to poor Lord Cronshaw to keep for me.'

'That was after supper?'

'Yes.'

'Not long before the tragedy, perhaps?'

A faint look of alarm came into Mrs Davidson's pale eyes, and she replied quickly: 'Oh no – long before that. Quite soon after supper, in fact.'

'I see. Well, that is all. I will not derange you further. *Bonjour, madame*.'

'Well,' I said as we emerged from the building, 'that explains the mystery of the green pompon.'

'I wonder.'

'Why, what do you mean?'

'You saw me examine the dress, Hastings?'

'Yes?'

'*Eh bien*, the pompon that was missing had not been wrenched off, as the lady said. On the contrary, it had been *cut* off, my friend, cut off with scissors. The threads were all quite even.'

'Dear me!' I exclaimed. 'This becomes more and more involved.'

'On the contrary,' replied Poirot placidly, 'it becomes more and more simple.'

'Poirot,' I cried, 'one day I shall murder you! Your habit of finding everything perfectly simple is aggravating to the last degree!'

'But when I explain, *mon ami*, is it not always perfectly simple?'

'Yes; that is the annoying part of it! I feel then that I could have done it myself.'

'And so you could, Hastings, so you could. If you would but take the trouble of arranging your ideas! Without method – '

'Yes, yes,' I said hastily, for I knew Poirot's eloquence when started on his favourite theme only too well. 'Tell me, what do we do next? Are you really going to reconstruct the crime?'

'Hardly that. Shall we say that the drama is over, but that I propose to add a – harlequinade?'

The following Tuesday was fixed upon by Poirot as the day for this mysterious performance. The preparations greatly intrigued me. A white screen was erected at one side of the room, flanked by heavy curtains at either side. A man with some lighting apparatus arrived next, and finally a group of members of the theatrical profession, who disappeared into Poirot's bedroom, which had been rigged up as a temporary dressing-room.

Shortly before eight, Japp arrived, in no very cheerful mood.

17

I gathered that the official detective hardly approved of Poirot's plan.

'Bit melodramatic, like all his ideas. But there, it can do no harm, and as he says, it might save us a good bit of trouble. He's been very smart over the case. I was on the same scent myself, of course –' I felt instinctively that Japp was straining the truth here – 'but there, I promised to let him play the thing out his own way. Ah! Here is the crowd.'

His Lordship arrived first, escorting Mrs Mallaby, whom I had not as yet seen. She was a pretty, dark-haired woman, and appeared perceptibly nervous. The Davidsons followed. Chris Davidson also I saw for the first time. He was handsome enough in a rather obvious style, tall and dark, with the easy grace of the actor.

Poirot had arranged seats for the party facing the screen. This was illuminated by a bright light. Poirot switched out the other lights so that the room was in darkness except for the screen. Poirot's voice rose out of the gloom.

'Messieurs, mesdames, a word of explanation. Six figures in turn will pass across the screen. They are familiar to you. Pierrot and his Pierrette; Punchinello the buffoon, and elegant Pulcinella; beautiful Columbine, lightly dancing, Harlequin, the sprite, invisible to man!'

With these words of introduction, the show began. In turn each figure that Poirot had mentioned bounded before the screen, stayed there a moment poised, and then vanished. The lights went up, and a sigh of relief went round. Everyone had been nervous, fearing they knew not what. It seemed to me that the proceedings had gone singularly flat. If the criminal was among us, and Poirot expected him to break down at the mere sight of a familiar figure the device had failed signally – as it was almost bound to do. Poirot, however, appeared not a whit discomposed. He stepped forward, beaming.

'Now, messieurs and mesdames, will you be so good as to tell me, one at a time, what it is that we have just seen? Will you begin, milor'?'

The gentleman looked rather puzzled. 'I'm afraid I don't quite understand.'

18

'Just tell me what we have been seeing.'

'I – er – well, I should say we have seen six figures passing in front of a screen and dressed to represent the personages in the old Italian Comedy, or – er – ourselves the other night.'

'Never mind the other night, milor',' broke in Poirot. 'The first part of your speech was what I wanted. Madame, you agree with Milor' Cronshaw?'

He had turned as he spoke to Mrs Mallaby.

'I – er – yes, of course.'

'You agree that you have seen six figures representing the Italian Comedy?'

'Why, certainly.'

'Monsieur Davidson? You too?'

'Yes.'

'Madame?'

'Yes.'

'Hastings? Japp? Yes? You are all in accord?'

He looked around upon us; his face grew rather pale, and his eyes were green as any cat's.

'And yet – *you are all wrong*! Your eyes have lied to you – as they lied to you on the night of the Victory Ball. To "see" things with your eyes, as they say, is not always to see the truth. One must see with the eyes of the mind; one must employ the little cells of grey! Know, then, that tonight and on the night of the Victory Ball, you saw not *six* figures but *five*! See!'

The lights went out again. A figure bounded in front of the screen – Pierrot!

'Who is that?' demanded Poirot. 'Is it Pierrot?'

'Yes,' we all cried.

'Look again!'

With a swift movement the man divested himself of his loose Pierrot garb. There in the limelight stood glittering Harlequin! At the same moment there was a cry and an overturned chair.

'Curse you,' snarled Davidson's voice. 'Curse you! How did you guess?'

Then came the clink of handcuffs and Japp's calm official voice. 'I arrest you, Christopher Davidson – charge of murdering Viscount Cronshaw – anything you say will be used in evidence against you.'

It was a quarter of an hour later. A recherché little supper had appeared; and Poirot, beaming all over his face, was dispensing hospitality and answering our eager questions.

'It was all very simple. The circumstances in which the green pompon was found suggested at once that it had been torn from the costume of the murderer. I dismissed Pierrette from my mind (since it takes considerable strength to drive a table-knife home) and fixed upon Pierrot as the criminal. But Pierrot left the ball nearly two hours before the murder was committed. So he must either have returned to the ball later to kill Lord Cronshaw, or – *eh bien*, he must have killed him before he left! Was that impossible? Who had seen Lord Cronshaw after supper that evening? Only Mrs Davidson, whose statement, I suspected, was a deliberate fabrication uttered with the object of accounting for the missing pompon, which, of course, she cut from her own dress to replace the one missing on her husband's costume. But then, Harlequin, who was seen in the box at one-thirty, must have been an impersonation. For a moment, earlier, I had considered the possibility of Mr Beltane being the guilty party. But with his elaborate costume, it was clearly impossible that he could have doubled the roles of Punchinello and Harlequin. On the other hand, to Davidson, a young man of about the same height as the murdered man and an actor by profession, the thing was simplicity itself.

'But one thing worried me. Surely a doctor could not fail to perceive the difference between a man who had been dead two hours and one who had been dead ten minutes! *Eh bien*, the doctor *did* perceive it! But he was not taken to the body and asked, 'How long has this man been dead?' On the contrary, he was informed that the man had been seen alive ten minutes ago, and so he merely commented at the inquest on the abnormal stiffening of the limbs for which he was quite unable to account!

'All was now marching famously for my theory. Davidson had killed Lord Cronshaw immediately after supper, when, as

20

you remember, he was seen to draw him back into the supper-room. Then he departed with Miss Courtenay, left her at the door of her flat (instead of going in and trying to pacify her as he affirmed) and returned post-haste to the Colossus – but as Harlequin, not Pierrot – a simple transformation effected by removing his outer costume.'

The uncle of the dead man leaned forward, his eyes perplexed.

'But if so, he must have come to the ball prepared to kill his victim. What earthly motive could he have had? The motive, that's what I can't get.'

'Ah! There we come to the second tragedy – that of Miss Courtenay. There was one simple point which everyone overlooked. Miss Courtenay died of cocaine poisoning – but her supply of the drug was in the enamel box which was found on Lord Cronshaw's body. Where, then, did she obtain the dose which killed her? Only one person could have supplied her with it – Davidson. And that explains everything. It accounts for her friendship with the Davidsons and her demand that Davidson should escort her home. Lord Cronshaw, who was almost fanatically opposed to drug-taking, discovered that she was addicted to cocaine, and suspected that Davidson supplied her with it. Davidson doubtless denied this, but Lord Cronshaw determined to get the truth from Miss Courtenay at the ball. He could forgive the wretched girl, but he would certainly have no mercy on the man who made a living by trafficking in drugs. Exposure and ruin confronted Davidson. He went to the ball determined that Cronshaw's silence must be obtained at any cost.'

'Was Coco's death an accident, then?'

'I suspect that it was an accident cleverly engineered by Davidson. She was furiously angry with Cronshaw, first for his reproaches, and secondly for taking her cocaine from her. Davidson supplied her with more, and probably suggested her augmenting the dose as a defiance to "old Cronch"!'

'One other thing,' I said. 'The recess and the curtain? How did you know about them?'

'Why, *mon ami*, that was the most simple of all. Waiters had been in and out of that little room, so, obviously, the body could not have been lying where it was found on the floor. There must be some place in the room where it could be hidden. I deduced a curtain and a recess behind it. Davidson dragged the body there, and later, after drawing attention to himself in the box, he dragged it out again before finally leaving the Hall. It was one of his best moves. He is a clever fellow!'

But in Poirot's green eyes I read unmistakably the unspoken remark: 'But not quite so clever as Hercule Poirot!'

THE ADVENTURE OF THE CLAPHAM COOK

At the time that I was sharing rooms with my friend Hercule Poirot, it was my custom to read aloud to him the headlines in the morning newspaper, the *Daily Blare*.

The *Daily Blare* was a paper that made the most of any opportunity for sensationalism. Robberies and murders did not lurk obscurely in its back pages. Instead they hit you in the eye in large type on the front page.

ABSCONDING BANK CLERK DISAPPEARS WITH FIFTY THOU-SAND POUNDS' WORTH OF NEGOTIABLE SECURITIES, I read.

HUSBAND PUTS HIS HEAD IN GAS-OVEN. UNHAPPY HOME LIFE. MISSING TYPIST. PRETTY GIRL OF TWENTY-ONE. WHERE IS EDNA FIELD?

'There you are, Poirot, plenty to choose from. An absconding bank clerk, a mysterious suicide, a missing typist – which will you have?'

My friend was in a placid mood. He quietly shook his head.

'I am not greatly attracted to any of them, *mon ami*. Today I feel inclined for the life of ease. It would have to be a very interesting problem to tempt me from my chair. See you, I have affairs of importance of my own to attend to.'

'Such as?'

'My wardrobe, Hastings. If I mistake not, there is on my new grey suit the spot of grease – only the unique spot, but it is sufficient to trouble me. Then there is my winter overcoat – I must lay him aside in the powder of Keatings. And I think – yes, I think – the moment is ripe for the trimmings of my moustaches – and afterwards I must apply the pomade.'

'Well,' I said, strolling to the window, 'I doubt if you'll be able to carry out this delirious programme. That was a ring at the bell. You have a client.'

'Unless the affair is one of national importance, I touch it not,' declared Poirot with dignity.

A moment later our privacy was invaded by a stout redfaced lady who panted audibly as a result of her rapid ascent of the stairs.

'You're M. Poirot?' she demanded, as she sank into a chair.

'I am Hercule Poirot, yes, madame.'

'You're not a bit like what I thought you'd be,' said the lady, eyeing him with some disfavour. 'Did you pay for the bit in the paper saying what a clever detective you were, or did they put it in themselves?'

'Madame!' said Poirot, drawing himself up.

'I'm sorry, I'm sure, but you know what these papers are nowadays. You begin reading a nice article "What a bride said to her plain unmarried friend", and it's all about a simple thing you buy at the chemist's and shampoo your hair with. Nothing but puff. But no offence taken, I hope? I'll tell you what I want you to do for me. I want you to find my cook.'

Poirot stared at her; for once his ready tongue failed him. I turned aside to hide the broadening smile I could not control.

'It's all this wicked dole,' continued the lady. 'Putting ideas into servants' heads, wanting to be typists and what nots. Stop the dole, that's what I say. I'd like to know what *my* servants have to complain of – afternoon and evening off a week, alternate Sundays, washing put out, same food as we have – and never a bit of margarine in the house, nothing but the very best butter.'

She paused for want of breath and Poirot seized his opportunity. He spoke in his haughtiest manner, rising to his feet as he did so.

'I fear you are making a mistake, madame. I am not holding an inquiry into the conditions of domestic service. I am a private detective.'

'I know that,' said our visitor. 'Didn't I tell you I wanted you to find my cook for me? Walked out of the house on Wednesday, without so much as a word to me, and never came back.'

'I am sorry, madame, but I do not touch this particular kind of business. I wish you good morning.'

Our visitor snorted with indignation.

'That's it, is it, my fine fellow? Too proud, eh? Only deal with Government secrets and countesses' jewels? Let me tell you a servant's every bit as important as a tiara to a woman in my position. We can't all be fine ladies going out in our motors with our diamonds and our pearls. A good cook's a good cook – and when you lose her, it's as much to you as her pearls are to some fine lady.'

For a moment or two it appeared to be a toss up between Poirot's dignity and his sense of humour. Finally he laughed and sat down again.

'Madame, you are in the right, and I am in the wrong. Your remarks are just and intelligent. This case will be a novelty. Never yet have I hunted a missing domestic. Truly here is the problem of national importance that I was demanding of fate just before your arrival. *En avant*! You say this jewel of a cook went out on Wednesday and did not return. That is the day before yesterday.'

'Yes, it was her day out.'

'But probably, madame, she has met with some accident. Have you inquired at any of the hospitals?'

'That's exactly what I thought yesterday, but this morning, if you please, she sent for her box. And not so much as a line to me! If I'd been at home, I'd not have let it go – treating me like that! But I'd just stepped out to the butcher.'

'Will you describe her to me?'

'She was middle-aged, stout, black hair turning grey – most respectable. She'd been ten years in her last place. Eliza Dunn, her name was.'

'And you had had – no disagreement with her on the Wednesday?'

'None whatsoever. That's what makes it all so queer.'

'How many servants do you keep, madame?'

'Two. The house-parlourmaid, Annie, is a very nice girl. A bit forgetful and her head full of young men, but a good servant if you keep her up to her work.'

'Did she and the cook get on well together?'

'They had their ups and downs, of course – but on the whole, very well.'

'And the girl can throw no light on the mystery?'

'She says not – but you know what servants are – they all hang together.'

'Well, well, we must look into this. Where did you say you resided, madame?'

'At Clapham; 88 Prince Albert Road.'

'*Bien*, madame, I will wish you good morning, and you may count upon seeing me at your residence during the course of the day.'

Mrs Todd, for such was our new friend's name, then took her departure. Poirot looked at me somewhat ruefully.

'Well, well, Hastings, this is a novel affair that we have here. The Disappearance of the Clapham Cook! Never, *never*, must our friend Inspector Japp get to hear of this!'

He then proceeded to heat an iron and carefully removed the grease spot from his grey suit by means of a piece of blotting-paper. His moustaches he regretfully postponed to another day, and we set out for Clapham.

Prince Albert Road proved to be a street of small prim houses, all exactly alike, with neat lace curtains veiling the windows, and well-polished brass knockers on the doors.

We rang the bell at No. 88, and the door was opened by a neat maid with a pretty face. Mrs Todd came out in the hall to greet us.

'Don't go, Annie,' she cried. 'This gentleman's a detective and he'll want to ask you some questions.'

Annie's face displayed a struggle between alarm and a pleasurable excitement.

'I thank you, madame,' said Poirot bowing. 'I would like to question your maid now – and to see her alone, if I may.'

We were shown into a small drawing-room, and when Mrs Todd, with obvious reluctance, had left the room, Poirot commenced his cross-examination.

'*Voyons, Mademoiselle Annie*, all that you shall tell us will be of the greatest importance. You alone can shed any light on the case. Without your assistance I can do nothing.'

The alarm vanished from the girl's face and the pleasurable excitement became more strongly marked.

'I'm sure, sir,' she said, 'I'll tell you anything I can.'

'That is good.' Poirot beamed approval on her. 'Now, first of all what is your own idea? You are a girl of remarkable intelligence. That can be seen at once! What is your own explanation of Eliza's disappearance?'

Thus encouraged, Annie fairly flowed into excited speech.

'White slavers, sir, I've said so all along! Cook was always warning me against them. "Don't you sniff no scent, or eat any sweets – no matter how gentlemanly the fellow!" Those were her words to me. And now they've got her! I'm sure of it. As likely as not, she's been shipped to Turkey or one of them Eastern places where I've heard they like them fat!'

Poirot preserved an admirable gravity.

'But in that case – and it is indeed an idea! – would she have sent for her trunk?'

'Well, I don't know, sir. She'd want her things – even in those foreign places.'

'Who came for the trunk – a man?'

'It was Carter Paterson, sir.'

'Did you pack it?'

'No, sir, it was already packed and corded.'

'Ah! That's interesting. That shows that when she left the house on Wednesday, she had already determined not to return. You see that, do you not?'

'Yes, sir.' Annie looked slightly taken aback. 'I hadn't thought of that. But it might still have been white slavers, mightn't it, sir? she added wistfully.

'Undoubtedly!' said Poirot gravely. He went on: 'Did you both occupy the same bedroom?'

'No, sir, we had separate rooms.'

'And had Eliza expressed any dissatisfaction with her present post to you at all? Were you both happy here?'

'She'd never mentioned leaving. The place is all right – ' The girl hesitated.

27

'Speak freely,' said Poirot kindly. 'I shall not tell your mistress.'

'Well, of course, sir, she's a caution, Missus is. But the food's good. Plenty of it, and no stinting. Something hot for supper, good outings, and as much frying-fat as you like. And anyway, if Eliza did want to make a change, she'd never have gone off this way, I'm sure. She'd have stayed her month. Why, Missus could have a month's wages out of her for doing this!'

'And the work, it is not too hard?'

'Well, she's particular – always poking round in corners and looking for dust. And then there's the lodger, or paying guest as he's always called. But that's only breakfast and dinner, same as Master. They're out all day in the City.'

'You like your master?'

'He's all right – very quiet and a bit on the stingy side.'

'You can't remember, I suppose, the last thing Eliza said before she went out?'

'Yes, I can. "If there's any stewed peaches over from the dining-room," she says, "we'll have them for supper, and a bit of bacon and some fried potatoes." Mad over stewed peaches, she was. I shouldn't wonder if they didn't get her that way.'

'Was Wednesday her regular day out?'

'Yes, she had Wednesdays and I had Thursdays.'

Poirot asked a few more questions, then declared himself satisfied. Annie departed, and Mrs Todd hurried in, her face alight with curiosity. She had, I felt certain, bitterly resented her exclusion from the room during our conversation with Annie. Poirot, however, was careful to soothe her feelings tactfully.

'It is difficult,' he explained, 'for a woman of exceptional intelligence such as yourself, madame, to bear patiently the roundabout methods we poor detectives are forced to use. To have patience with stupidity is difficult for the quick-witted.'

Having thus charmed away any little resentment on Mrs Todd's part, he brought the conversation round to her husband and elicited the information that he worked with a firm in the City and would not be home until after six.

'Doubtless he is very disturbed and worried by this unaccountable business, eh? Is it not so?'

'He's never worried,' declared Mrs Todd. ' "Well, well, get another, my dear." That's all *he* said! He's so calm that it drives me to distraction sometimes. "An ungrateful woman," he said. "We are well rid of her." '

'What about the other inmates of the house, madame?'

'You mean Mr Simpson, our paying guest? Well, as long as he gets his breakfast and his evening meal all right, *he* doesn't worry.'

'What is his profession, madame?'

'He works in a bank.' She mentioned its name, and I started slightly, remembering my perusal of the *Daily Blare*.

'A young man?'

'Twenty-eight, I believe. Nice quiet young fellow.'

'I should like to have a few words with him, and also with your husband, if I may. I will return for that purpose this evening. I venture to suggest that you should repose yourself a little, madame, you look fatigued.'

'I should just think I am! First the worry about Eliza, and then I was at the sales practically all yesterday, and you know what *that* is, M. Poirot, and what with one thing and another and a lot to do in the house, because of course Annie can't do it all – and very likely she'll give notice anyway, being unsettled in this way – well, what with it all, I'm tired out!'

Poirot murmured sympathetically, and we took our leave.

'It's a curious coincidence,' I said, 'but that absconding clerk, Davis, was from the same bank as Simpson. Can there be any connection, do you think?'

Poirot smiled.

'At the one end, a defaulting clerk, at the other a vanishing cook. It is hard to see any relation between the two, unless possibly Davis visited Simpson, fell in love with the cook, and persuaded her to accompany him on his flight!'

I laughed. But Poirot remained grave.

'He might have done worse,' he said reprovingly. 'Remember, Hastings, if you are going into exile, a good cook may be of more comfort than a pretty face!' He paused for a moment and then went on. 'It is a curious case, full of contradictory features. I am interested – yes, I am distinctly interested.'

That evening we returned to 88 Prince Albert Road and interviewed both Todd and Simpson. The former was a melancholy lantern-jawed man of forty-odd.

'Oh! Yes, yes,' he said vaguely. 'Eliza. Yes. A good cook, I believe. And economical. I make a strong point of economy.'

'Can you imagine any reason for her leaving you so suddenly?'

'Oh, well,' said Mr Todd vaguely. 'Servants, you know. My wife worries too much. Worn out from always worrying. The whole problem's quite simple really. "Get another, my dear," I say. "Get another." That's all there is to it. No good crying over spilt milk.'

Mr Simpson was equally unhelpful. He was a quiet inconspicuous young man with spectacles.

'I must have seen her, I suppose,' he said. 'Elderly woman, wasn't she? Of course, it's the other one I see always, Annie. Nice girl. Very obliging.'

'Were those two on good terms with each other?'

Mr Simpson said he couldn't say, he was sure. He supposed so.

'Well, we get nothing of interest there, *mon ami*,' said Poirot as we left the house. Our departure had been delayed by a burst of vociferous repetition from Mrs Todd, who repeated everything she had said that morning at rather greater length.

'Are you disappointed?' I asked. 'Did you expect to hear something?'

Poirot shook his head.

'There was a possibility, of course,' he said. 'But I hardly thought it likely.'

The next development was a letter which Poirot received on the following morning. He read it, turned purple with indignation, and handed it to me.

Mrs Todd regrets that after all she will not avail herself

30

of Mr Poirot's services. After talking the matter over with her husband she sees that it is foolish to call in a detective about a purely domestic affair. Mrs Todd encloses a guinea for consultation fee.

'Aha!' cried Poirot angrily. 'And they think to get rid of Hercule Poirot like that! As a favour – a great favour – I consent to investigate their miserable little twopenny-halfpenny affair – and they dismiss me *comme ça*! Here, I mistake not, is the hand of Mr Todd. But I say no! – thirty-six times no! I will spend my own guineas, thirty-six hundred of them if need be, but I will get to the bottom of this matter!'

'Yes,' I said. 'But how?'

Poirot calmed down a little.

'*D'abord*,' he said, 'we will advertise in the papers. Let me see – yes – something like this: "If Eliza Dunn will communicate with this address, she will hear of something to her advantage.' Put it in all the papers you can think of, Hastings. Then I will make some little inquiries of my own. Go, go – all must be done as quickly as possible!'

I did not see him again until the evening, when he condescended to tell me what he had been doing.

'I have made inquiries at the firm of Mr Todd. He was not absent on Wednesday, and he bears a good character – so much for him. Then Simpson, on Thursday he was ill and did not come to the bank, but he was there on Wednesday. He was moderately friendly with Davis. Nothing out of the common. There does not seem to be anything there. No. We must place our reliance on the advertisement.'

The advertisement duly appeared in all the principal daily papers. By Poirot's orders it was to be continued every day for a week. His eagerness over this uninteresting matter of a defaulting cook was extraordinary, but I realized that he considered it a point of honour to persevere until he finally succeeded. Several extremely interesting cases were brought to him about this time, but he declined them all. Every morning he would rush at his letters, scrutinize them earnestly and then lay them down with a sigh.

But our patience was rewarded at last. On the Wednesday following Mrs Todd's visit, our landlady informed us that a person of the name of Eliza Dunn had called.

'*Enfin!*' cried Poirot. 'But make her mount then! At once. Immediately.'

Thus admonished, our landlady hurried out and returned a moment or two later, ushering in Miss Dunn. Our quarry was much as described: tall, stout, and eminently respectable.

'I came in answer to the advertisement,' she explained. 'I thought there must be some muddle or other, and that perhaps you didn't know I'd already got my legacy.'

Poirot was studying her attentively. He drew forward a chair with a flourish.

'The truth of the matter is,' he explained, 'that your late mistress, Mrs Todd, was much concerned about you. She feared some accident might have befallen you.'

Eliza Dunn seemed very much surprised.

'Didn't she get my letter then?'

'She got no word of any kind.' He paused, and then said persuasively: 'Recount to me the whole story, will you not?'

Eliza Dunn needed no encouragement. She plunged at once into a lengthy narrative.

'I was just coming home on Wednesday night and had nearly got to the house, when a gentleman stopped me. A tall gentleman he was, with a beard and a big hat. "Miss Eliza Dunn?" he said. "Yes," I said. "I've been inquiring for you at No. 88," he said. "They told me I might meet you coming along here. Miss Dunn, I have come from Australia specially to find you. Do you happen to know the maiden name of your maternal grandmother?" "Jane Emmott," I said. "Exactly," he said. "Now, Miss Dunn, although you may never have heard of the fact, your grandmother had a great friend, Eliza Leech. This friend went to Australia where she married a very wealthy settler. Her two children died in infancy, and she inherited all her husband's property. She died a few months ago, and by her will you inherit a house in this country and a considerable sum of money."

'You could have knocked me down with a feather,' continued Miss Dunn. 'For a minute, I was suspicious, and he must have seen it, for he smiled. "Quite right to be on your guard, Miss Dunn," he said. "Here are my credentials." He handed me a letter from some lawyers in Melbourne, Hurst and Crotchet, and a card. He was Mr Crotchet. "There are one or two conditions," he said. "Our client was a little eccentric, you know. The bequest is conditional on your taking possession of the house (it is in Cumberland) before twelve o'clock tomorrow. The other condition is of no importance – it is merely a stipulation that you should not be in domestic service." My face fell. "Oh, Mr Crotchet," I said. "I'm a cook. Didn't they tell you at the house?" "Dear, dear," he said. "I had no idea of such a thing. I thought you might possibly be a companion or governess there. This is very unfortunate – very unfortunate indeed."

' "Shall I have to lose all the money?" I said, anxious like. He thought for a minute or two. "There are always ways of getting round the law, Miss Dunn," he said at last. "We as lawyers know that. The way out here is for you to have left your employment this afternoon." "But my month?" I said. "My dear Miss Dunn," he said with a smile. "You can leave an employer any minute by forfeiting a month's wages. Your mistress will understand in view of the circumstances. The difficulty is *time*! It is imperative that you should catch the 11.5 from King's Cross to the north. I can advance you ten pounds or so for the fare, and you can write a note at the station to your employer. I will take it to her myself and explain the whole circumstances." I agreed, of course, and an hour later I was in the train, so flustered that I didn't know whether I was on my head or heels. Indeed by the time I got to Carlisle, I was half inclined to think the whole thing was one of those confidence tricks you read about. But I went to the address he had given me – solicitors they were, and it was all right. A nice little house, and an income of three hundred a year. These lawyers knew very little, they'd just got a letter from a gentleman in London instructing them to hand over the house to me and £150 for the first six months. Mr Crotchet sent up my things to me, but there was no word from Missus. I supposed she was

33

angry and grudged me my bit of luck. She kept back my box too, and sent my clothes in paper parcels. But there, of course if she never had my letter, she might think it a bit cool of me.'

Poirot had listened attentively to this long history. Now he nodded his head as though completely satisfied.

'Thank you, mademoiselle. There had been, as you say, a little muddle. Permit me to recompense you for your trouble.' He handed her an envelope. 'You return to Cumberland immediately? A little word in your ear. *Do not forget how to cook*. It is always useful to have something to fall back upon in case things go wrong.'

'Credulous,' he murmured, as our visitor departed, 'but perhaps not more than most of her class.' His face grew grave. 'Come, Hastings, there is no time to be lost. Get a taxi while I write a note to Japp.'

Poirot was waiting on the doorstep when I returned with the taxi.

'Where are we going?' I asked anxiously.

'First, to despatch this note by special messenger.'

This was done, and re-entering the taxi Poirot gave the address to the driver.

'Eighty-eight Prince Albert Road, Clapham.'

'So we are going there?'

'*Mais oui*. Though frankly I fear we shall be too late. Our bird will have flown, Hastings.'

'Who is our bird?'

Poirot smiled.

'The inconspicuous Mr Simpson.'

'What?' I exclaimed.

'Oh, come now, Hastings, do not tell me that all is not clear to you now!'

'The cook was got out of the way, I realize that,' I said, slightly piqued. 'But why? *Why* should Simpson wish to get her out of the house? Did she know something about him?'

'Nothing whatever.'

'Well, then – '

'But he wanted something that she had.'

'Money? The Australian legacy?'

34

'No, my friend – something quite different.' He paused a moment and then said gravely: '*A battered tin trunk . . .*'

I looked sideways at him. His statement seemed so fantastic that I suspected him of pulling my leg, but he was perfectly grave and serious.

'Surely he could buy a trunk if he wanted one,' I cried.

'He did not want a new trunk. He wanted a trunk of pedigree. A trunk of assured respectability.'

'Look here, Poirot,' I cried, 'this really is a bit thick. You're pulling my leg.'

He looked at me.

'You lack the brains and the imagination of Mr Simpson, Hastings. See here: On Wednesday evening, Simpson decoys away the cook. A printed card and a printed sheet of notepaper are simple matters to obtain, and he is willing to pay £150 and a year's house rent to assure the success of his plan. Miss Dunn does not recognize him – the beard and the hat and the slight colonial accent completely deceive her. That is the end of Wednesday – except for the trifling fact that Simpson has helped himself to fifty thousand pounds' worth of negotiable securities.'

'*Simpson* – but it was *Davis* – '

'If you will kindly permit me to continue, Hastings! Simpson knows that the theft will be discovered on Thursday afternoon. He does not go to the bank on Thursday, but he lies in wait for Davis when he comes out to lunch. Perhaps he admits the theft and tells Davis he will return the securities to him – anyhow he succeeds in getting Davis to come to Clapham with him. It is the maid's day out, and Mrs Todd was at the sales, so there is no one in the house. When the theft is discovered and Davis is missing, the implication will be overwhelming. Davis is the thief! Mr Simpson will be perfectly safe, and can return to work on the morrow like the honest clerk they think him.'

'And Davis?'

Poirot made an expressive gesture, and slowly shook his head.

'It seems too cold-blooded to be believed, and yet what other explanation can there be, *mon ami*. The one difficulty for a murderer is the disposal of the body – and Simpson had planned that out beforehand. I was struck at once by the fact that although Eliza Dunn obviously meant to return that night when she went out (witness her remark about the stewed peaches) *yet her trunk was all ready packed when they came for it*. It was Simpson who sent word to Carter Paterson to call on Friday and it was Simpson who corded up the box on Thursday afternoon. What suspicion could possibly arise? A maid leaves and sends for her box, it is labelled and addressed ready in her name, probably to a railway station within easy reach of London. On Saturday afternoon, Simpson, in his Australian disguise, claims it, he affixes a new label and address and redespatches it somewhere else, again "to be left till called for". When the authorities get suspicious, for excellent reasons, and open it, all that can be elicited will be that a bearded colonial despatched it from some junction near London. There will be nothing to connect it with 88 Prince Albert Road. Ah! Here we are.'

Poirot's prognostications had been correct. Simpson had left days previously. But he was not to escape the consequences of his crime. By the aid of wireless, he was discovered on the *Olympia*, en route to America.

A tin trunk, addressed to Mr Henry Wintergreen, attracted the attention of railway officials at Glasgow. It was opened and found to contain the body of the unfortunate Davis.

Mrs Todd's cheque for a guinea was never cashed. Instead Poirot had it framed and hung on the wall of our sitting-room.

'It is to me a little reminder, Hastings. Never to despise the trivial – the undignified. A disappearing domestic at one end – a cold-blooded murder at the other. To me, one of the most interesting of my cases.'

'Mrs Pengelley,' announced our landlady, and withdrew discreetly.

Many unlikely people came to consult Poirot, but to my mind, the woman who stood nervously just inside the door, fingering her feather neck-piece, was the most unlikely of all. She was so extraordinarily commonplace – a thin, faded woman of about fifty, dressed in a braided coat and skirt, some gold jewellery at her neck, and with her grey hair surmounted by a singularly unbecoming hat. In a country town you pass a hundred Mrs Pengelleys in the street every day.

Poirot came forward and greeted her pleasantly, perceiving her obvious embarrassment.

'Madame! Take a chair, I beg of you. My colleague, Captain Hastings.'

The lady sat down, murmuring uncertainly: 'You are M. Poirot, the detective?'

'At your service, madame.'

But our guest was still tongue-tied. She sighed, twisted her fingers, and grew steadily redder and redder.

'There is something I can do for you, eh, madame?'

'Well, I thought – that is – you see – '

'Proceed, madame, I beg of you – proceed.'

Mrs Pengelley, thus encouraged, took a grip on herself.

'It's this way, M. Poirot – I don't want to have anything to do with the police. No, I wouldn't go to the police for anything! But all the same, I'm sorely troubled about something. And yet I don't know if I ought – ' She stopped abruptly.

'Me, I have nothing to do with the police. My investigations are strictly private.'

Mrs Pengelley caught at the word.

'Private – that's what I want. I don't want any talk or fuss, or things in the papers. Wicked it is, the way they write things, until the family could never hold up their heads again. And it isn't as though I was even sure – it's just a dreadful idea that's come to me, and put it out of my head I can't.' She paused for breath. 'And all the time I may be wickedly wronging poor Edward. It's a terrible thought for any wife to have. But you do read of such dreadful things nowadays.'

'Permit me – it is of your husband you speak?'

'Yes.'

'And you suspect him of – what?'

'I don't like even to say it, M. Poirot. But you *do* read of such things happening – and the poor souls suspecting nothing.'

I was beginning to despair of the lady's ever coming to the point, but Poirot's patience was equal to the demand made upon it.

'Speak without fear, madame. Think what joy will be yours if we are able to prove your suspicions unfounded.'

'That's true – anything's better than this wearing uncertainty. Oh, M. Poirot, I'm dreadfully afraid I'm being *poisoned*.'

'What makes you think so?'

Mrs Pengelley, her reticence leaving her, plunged into a full recital more suited to the ears of her medical attendant.

'Pain and sickness after food, eh?' said Poirot thoughtfully. 'You have a doctor attending you, madame? What does he say?'

'He says it's acute gastritis, M. Poirot. But I can see that he's puzzled and uneasy, and he's always altering the medicine, but nothing does any good.'

'You have spoken of your – fears, to him?'

'No, indeed, M. Poirot. It might get about in the town. And perhaps it *is* gastritis. All the same, it's very odd that whenever Edward is away for the week-end, I'm quite all right again. Even Freda notices that – my niece, M. Poirot. And then there's that bottle of weed-killer, never used, the gardener says, and yet it's half-empty.'

She looked appealingly at Poirot. He smiled reassuringly at her, and reached for a pencil and notebook.

'Let us be businesslike, madame. Now, then, you and your husband reside – where?'

'Polgarwith, a small market town in Cornwall.'

'You have lived there long?'

'Fourteen years.'

'And your household consists of you and your husband. Any children?'

'No.'

'But a niece, I think you said?'

'Yes, Freda Stanton, the child of my husband's only sister. She has lived with us for the last eight years – that is, until a week ago.'

'Oh, and what happened a week ago?'

'Things hadn't been very pleasant for some time; I don't know what had come over Freda. She was so rude and impertinent, and her temper something shocking, and in the end she flared up one day, and out she walked and took rooms of her own in the town. I've not seen her since. Better leave her to come to her senses, so Mr Radnor says.'

'Who is Mr Radnor?'

Some of Mrs Pengelley's initial embarrassment returned.

'Oh, he's – he's just a friend. Very pleasant young fellow.'

'Anything between him and your niece?'

'Nothing whatever,' said Mrs Pengelley emphatically.

Poirot shifted his ground.

'You and your husband are, I presume, in comfortable circumstances?'

'Yes, we're very nicely off.'

'The money, is it yours or your husband's?'

'Oh, it's all Edward's. I've nothing of my own.'

'You see, madame, to be businesslike, we must be brutal. We must seek for a motive. Your husband, he would not poison you just *pour passer le temps*! Do you know of any reason why he should wish you out of the way?'

'There's the yellow-haired hussy who works for him,' said Mrs Pengelley, with a flash of temper. 'My husband's a dentist, M. Poirot, and nothing would do but he must have a smart girl, as he said, with bobbed hair and a white overall, to make his appointments and mix his fillings for him. It's come to my ears that there have been fine goings-on, though of course he swears it's all right.'

'This bottle of weed-killer, madame, who ordered it?'

'My husband – about a year ago.'

'Your niece, now, has she any money of her own?'

'About fifty pounds a year, I should say. She'd be glad enough to come back and keep house for Edward if I left him.'

'You have contemplated leaving him, then?'

'I don't intend to let him have it all his own way. Women aren't the downtrodden slaves they were in the old days, M. Poirot.'

'I congratulate you on your independent spirit, madame; but let us be practical. You return to Polgarwith today?'

'Yes, I came up by an excursion. Six this morning the train started, and the train goes back at five this afternoon.'

'*Bien*! I have nothing of great moment on hand. I can devote myself to your little affair. Tomorrow I shall be in Polgarwith. Shall we say that Hastings, here, is a distant relative of yours, the son of your second cousin? Me, I am his eccentric foreign friend. In the meantime, eat only what is prepared by your own hands, or under your eye. You have a maid whom you trust?'

'Jessie is a very good girl, I am sure.'

'Till tomorrow then, madame, and be of good courage.'

Poirot bowed the lady out, and returned thoughtfully to his chair. His absorption was not so great, however, that he failed to see two minute strands of feather scarf wrenched off by the lady's agitated fingers. He collected them carefully and consigned them to the wastepaper basket.

'What do you make of the case, Hastings?'

'A nasty business, I should say.'

'Yes, if what the lady suspects be true. But is it? Woe betide any husband who orders a bottle of weed-killer nowadays. If his wife suffers from gastritis, and is inclined to be of a hysterical temperament, the fat is in the fire.'

'You think that is all there is to it?'

'Ah – *voilà* – I do not know, Hastings. But the case interests me – it interests me enormously. For, you see, it has positively no new features. Hence the hysterical theory, and yet Mrs Pengelley did not strike me as being a hysterical woman. Yes, if I mistake not, we have here a very poignant human drama. Tell me, Hastings, what do you consider Mrs Pengelley's feelings towards her husband to be?'

'Loyalty struggling with fear,' I suggested.

'Yet, ordinarily, a woman will accuse anyone in the world – but not her husband. She will stick to her belief in him through thick and thin.'

'The "other woman" complicates the matter.'

'Yes, affection may turn to hate, under the stimulus of jealousy. But hate would take her to the police – not to me. She would want an outcry – a scandal. No, no, let us exercise our little grey cells. Why did she come to me? To have her suspicions proved wrong? Or – to have them *proved right*? Ah, we have here something I do not understand – an unknown factor. Is she a superb actress, our Mrs Pengelley? No, she was genuine, I would swear that she was genuine, and therefore I am interested. Look up the trains to Polgarwith, I pray you.'

The best train of the day was the one-fifty from Paddington which reached Polgarwith just after seven o'clock. The journey was uneventful, and I had to rouse myself from a pleasant nap to alight upon the platform of the bleak little station. We took our bags to the Duchy Hotel, and after a light meal, Poirot suggested our stepping round to pay an after-dinner call on my so-called cousin.

The Pengelleys' house stood a little way back from the road with an old-fashioned cottage garden in front. The smell of stocks and mignonette came sweetly wafted on the evening breeze. It seemed impossible to associate thoughts of violence with this Old World charm. Poirot rang and knocked. As the summons was not answered, he rang again. This time, after a little pause, the door was opened by a dishevelled-looking servant. Her eyes were red, and she was sniffing violently.

'We wish to see Mrs Pengelley,' explained Poirot. 'May we enter?'

The maid stared. Then, with unusual directness, she answered: 'Haven't you heard, then? She's dead. Died this evening – about half an hour ago.'

We stood staring at her, stunned.

'What did she die of?' I asked at last.

'There's some as could tell.' She gave a quick glance over her shoulder. 'If it wasn't that somebody ought to be in the house with the missus, I'd pack my box and go tonight. But I'll not leave her dead with no one to watch by her. It's not my place to say anything, and I'm not going to say anything – but everybody knows. It's all over the town. And if Mr Radnor don't write to the 'Ome Secretary, someone else will. The doctor may say what he likes. Didn't I see the master with my own eyes a-lifting down of the weed-killer from the shelf this very evening? And didn't he jump when he turned round and saw me watching of him? And the missus' gruel there on the table, all ready to take to her? Not another bit of food passes my lips while I am in this house! Not if I dies for it.'

'Where does the doctor live who attended your mistress?'

'Dr Adams. Round the corner in High Street. The second house.'

Poirot turned away abruptly. He was very pale.

'For a girl who was not going to say anything, that girl said a lot,' I remarked dryly.

Poirot struck his clenched hand into his palm.

'An imbecile, a criminal imbecile, that is what I have been, Hastings. I have boasted of my little grey cells, and now I have lost a human life, a life that came to me to be saved. Never did I dream that anything would happen so soon. May the good God forgive me, but I never believed anything would happen at all. Her story seemed to me artificial. Here we are at the doctor's. Let us see what he can tell us.'

Dr Adams was the typical genial red-faced country doctor of fiction. He received us politely enough, but at a hint of our errand, his red face became purple.

'Damned nonsense! Damned nonsense, every word of it! Wasn't I in attendance on the case? Gastritis – gastritis pure and simple. This town's a hotbed of gossip – a lot of scandal-mongering old women get together and invent God knows what. They read these scurrilous rags of newspapers, and nothing will suit them but that someone in their town shall get poisoned too. They see a bottle of weed-killer on a shelf – and hey presto! – away goes their imagination with the bit between his teeth. I know Edward Pengelley – he wouldn't poison his grandmother's dog. And why should he poison his wife? Tell me that?'

'There is one thing, M. le Docteur, that perhaps you do not know.'

And, very briefly, Poirot outlined the main facts of Mrs Pengelley's visit to him. No one could have been more astonished than Dr Adams. His eyes almost started out of his head.

'God bless my soul!' he ejaculated. 'The poor woman must have been mad. Why didn't she speak to me? That was the proper thing to do.'

'And have her fears ridiculed?'

'Not at all, not at all. I hope I've got an open mind.'

Poirot looked at him and smiled. The physician was evidently more perturbed than he cared to admit. As we left the house, Poirot broke into a laugh.

'He is as obstinate as a pig, that one. He has said it is gastritis; therefore it is gastritis! All the same, he has the mind uneasy.'

'What's our next step?'

'A return to the inn, and a night of horror upon one of your English provincial beds, *mon ami*. It is a thing to make pity, the cheap English bed!'

'And tomorrow?'

'*Rien à faire*. We must return to town and await developments.'

'That's very tame,' I said, disappointed. 'Suppose there are none?'

'There will be! I promise you that. Our old doctor may give as many certificates as he pleases. He cannot stop several hundred tongues from wagging. And they will wag to some purpose, I can tell you that!'

43

Our train for town left at eleven the following morning. Before we started for the station, Poirot expressed a wish to see Miss Freda Stanton, the niece mentioned to us by the dead woman. We found the house where she was lodging easily enough. With her was a tall, dark young man whom she introduced in some confusion as Mr Jacob Radnor.

Miss Freda Stanton was an extremely pretty girl of the old Cornish type – dark hair and eyes and rosy cheeks. There was a flash in those same dark eyes which told of a temper that it would not be wise to provoke.

'Poor Auntie,' she said, when Poirot had introduced himself, and explained his business. 'It's terribly sad. I've been wishing all the morning that I'd been kinder and more patient.'

'You stood a great deal, Freda,' interrupted Radnor.

'Yes, Jacob, but I've got a sharp temper, I know. After all, it was only silliness on Auntie's part. I ought to have just laughed and not minded. Of course, it's all nonsense her thinking that Uncle was poisoning her. She *was* worse after any food he gave her – but I'm sure it was only from thinking about it. She made up her mind she would be, and then she was.'

'What was the actual cause of your disagreement, mademoiselle?'

Miss Stanton hesitated, looking at Radnor. That young gentleman was quick to take the hint.

'I must be getting along, Freda. See you this evening. Goodbye, gentlemen; you're on your way to the station, I suppose?'

Poirot replied that we were, and Radnor departed.

'You are affianced, is it not so?' demanded Poirot, with a sly smile.

Freda Stanton blushed and admitted that such was the case.

'And that was really the whole trouble with Auntie,' she added.

'She did not approve of the match for you?'

'Oh, it wasn't that so much. But you see, she –' The girl came to a stop.

'Yes?' encouraged Poirot gently.

'It seems rather a horrid thing to say about her – now she's

44

dead. But you'll never understand unless I tell you. Auntie was absolutely infatuated with Jacob.'

'Indeed?'

'Yes, wasn't it absurd? She was over fifty, and he's not quite thirty! But there it was. She was silly about him! I had to tell her at last that it was me he was after – and she carried on dreadfully. She wouldn't believe a word of it, and was so rude and insulting that it's no wonder I lost my temper. I talked it over with Jacob, and we agreed that the best thing to do was for me to clear out for a bit till she came to her senses. Poor Auntie – I suppose she was in a queer state altogether.'

'It would certainly seem so. Thank you, mademoiselle, for making things so clear to me.'

A little to my surprise, Radnor was waiting for us in the street below.

'I can guess pretty well what Freda has been telling you,' he remarked. 'It was a most unfortunate thing to happen, and very awkward for me, as you can imagine. I need hardly say that it was none of my doing. I was pleased at first, because I imagined the old woman was helping on things with Freda. The whole thing was absurd – but extremely unpleasant.'

'When are you and Miss Stanton going to be married?'

'Soon, I hope. Now, M. Poirot, I'm going to be candid with you. I know a bit more than Freda does. She believes her uncle to be innocent. I'm not so sure. But I can tell you one thing: I'm going to keep my mouth shut about what I do know. Let sleeping dogs lie. I don't want my wife's uncle tried and hanged for murder.'

'Why do you tell me all this?'

'Because I've heard of you, and I know you're a clever man. It's quite possible that you might ferret out a case against him. But I put it to you – what good is that? The poor woman is past help, and she'd have been the last person to want a scandal – why, she'd turn in her grave at the mere thought of it.'

'You are probably right there. You want me to – hush it up, then?'

'That's my idea. I'll admit frankly that I'm selfish about it.

45

I've got my way to make – and I'm building up a good little business as a tailor and outfitter.'

'Most of us are selfish, Mr Radnor. Not all of us admit it so freely. I will do what you ask – but I tell you frankly you will not succeed in hushing it up.'

'Why not?'

Poirot held up a finger. It was market day, and we were passing the market – a busy hum came from within.

'The voice of the people – that is why, Mr Radnor. Ah, we must run, or we shall miss our train.'

'Very interesting, is it not, Hastings?' said Poirot, as the train steamed out of the station.

He had taken out a small comb from his pocket, also a microscopic mirror, and was carefully arranging his moustache, the symmetry of which had become slightly impaired during our brisk run.

'You seem to find it so,' I replied. 'To me, it is all rather sordid and unpleasant. There's hardly any mystery about it.'

'I agree with you; there is no mystery whatever.'

'I suppose we can accept the girl's rather extraordinary story of her aunt's infatuation? That seemed the only fishy part to me. She was such a nice, respectable woman.'

'There is nothing extraordinary about that – it is completely ordinary. If you read the papers carefully, you will find that often a nice respectable woman of that age leaves a husband she has lived with for twenty years, and sometimes a whole family of children as well, in order to link her life with that of a young man considerably her junior. You admire *les femmes*, Hastings; you prostrate yourself before all of them who are good-looking and have the good taste to smile upon you; but psychologically you know nothing whatever about them. In the autumn of a woman's life, there comes always one mad moment when she longs for romance, for adventure – before it is too late. It comes none the less surely to a woman because she is the wife of a respectable dentist in a country town!'

'And you think – '

'That a clever man might take advantage of such a moment.'

46

'I shouldn't call Pengelley so clever,' I mused. 'He's got the whole town by the ears. And yet I suppose you're right. The only two men who know anything, Radnor and the doctor, both want to hush it up. He's managed that somehow. I wish we'd seen the fellow.'

'You can indulge your wish. Return by the next train and invent an aching molar.'

I looked at him keenly.

'I wish I knew what you considered so interesting about the case.'

'My interest is very aptly summed up by a remark of yours, Hastings. After interviewing the maid, you observed that for someone who was not going to say a word, she had said a good deal.'

'Oh!' I said doubtfully; then I harped back to my original criticism: 'I wonder why you made no attempt to see Pengelley?'

'*Mon ami*, I give him just three months. Then I shall see him for as long as I please – in the dock.'

For once I thought Poirot's prognostications were going to be proved wrong. The time went by, and nothing transpired as to our Cornish case. Other matters occupied us, and I had nearly forgotten the Pengelley tragedy when it was suddenly recalled to me by a short paragraph in the paper which stated that an order to exhume the body of Mrs Pengelley had been obtained from the Home Secretary.

A few days later, and 'The Cornish Mystery' was the topic of every paper. It seemed that gossip had never entirely died down, and when the engagement of the widower to Miss Marks, his secretary, was announced, the tongues burst out again louder than ever. Finally a petition was sent to the Home Secretary; the body was exhumed; large quantities of arsenic were discovered; and Mr Pengelley was arrested and charged with the murder of his wife.

Poirot and I attended the preliminary proceedings. The evidence was much as might have been expected. Dr Adams admitted that the symptoms of arsenical poisoning might easily be mistaken for those of gastritis. The Home Office expert gave his evidence; the maid Jessie poured out a flood of voluble information, most of which was rejected, but which certainly strengthened the case against the prisoner. Freda Stanton gave evidence as to her aunt's being worse whenever she ate food prepared by her husband. Jacob Radnor told how he had dropped in unexpectedly on the day of Mrs Pengelley's death, and found Pengelley replacing the bottle of weed-killer on the pantry shelf, Mrs Pengelley's gruel being on the table close by. Then Miss Marks, the fair-haired secretary, was called, and wept and went into hysterics and admitted that there had been 'passages' between her and her employer, and that he had promised to marry her in the event of anything happening to his wife. Pengelley reserved his defence and was sent for trial.

Jacob Radnor walked back with us to our lodgings.

'You see, Mr Radnor,' said Poirot, 'I was right. The voice of the people spoke – and with no uncertain voice. There was to be no hushing up of this case.'

'You were quite right,' sighed Radnor. 'Do you see any chance of his getting off?'

'Well, he has reserved his defence. He may have something – up the sleeves, as you English say. Come in with us, will you not?'

Radnor accepted the invitation. I ordered two whiskies and sodas and a cup of chocolate. The last order caused consternation, and I much doubted whether it would ever put in an appearance.

'Of course,' continued Poirot, 'I have a good deal of experience in matters of this kind. And I see only one loophole of escape for our friend.'

'What is it?'

'That you should sign this paper.'

With the suddenness of a conjuror, he produced a sheet of paper covered with writing.

'What is it?'

'A confesssion that *you* murdered Mrs Pengelley.'

There was a moment's pause; then Radnor laughed.

48

'You must be mad!'

'No, no, my friend, I am not mad. You came here; you started a little business; you were short of money. Mr Pengelley was a man very well-to-do. You met his niece; she was inclined to smile upon you. But the small allowance that Pengelley might have given her upon her marriage was not enough for you. You must get rid of both the uncle and the aunt; then the money would come to her, since she was the only relative. How cleverly you set about it! You made love to that plain middle-aged woman until she was your slave. You implanted in her doubts of her husband. She discovered first that he was deceiving her – then, under your guidance, that he was trying to poison her. You were often at the house; you had opportunities to introduce the arsenic into her food. But you were careful never to do so when her husband was away. Being a woman, she did not keep her suspicions to herself. She talked to her niece; doubtless she talked to other women friends. Your only difficulty was keeping up separate relations with the two women, and even that was not so difficult as it looked. You explained to the aunt that, to allay the suspicions of her husband, you had to pretend to pay court to the niece. And the younger lady needed little convincing – she would never seriously consider her aunt as a rival.

'But then Mrs Pengelley made up her mind, without saying anything to you, to consult *me*. If she could be really assured, beyond any possible doubt, that her husband was trying to poison her, she would feel justified in leaving him, and linking her life with yours – which is what she imagined you wanted her to do. But that did not suit your book at all. You did not want a detective prying around. A favourable minute occurs. You are in the house when Mr Pengelley is getting some gruel for his wife, and you introduce the fatal dose. The rest is easy. Apparently anxious to hush matters up, you secretly foment them. But you reckoned without Hercule Poirot, my intelligent young friend.'

Radnor was deadly pale, but he still endeavoured to carry off matters with a high hand.

'Very interesting and ingenious, but why tell me all this?'

49

'Because, monsieur, I represent – not the law, but Mrs Pengelley. For her sake, I give you a chance of escape. Sign this paper, and you shall have twenty-four hours' start – twenty-four hours before I place it in the hands of the police.'

Radnor hesitated.

'You can't prove anything.'

'Can't I? I am Hercule Poirot. Look out of the window, monsieur. There are two men in the street. They have orders not to lose sight of you.'

Radnor strode across to the window and pulled aside the blind, then shrank back with an oath.

'You see, monsieur? Sign – it is your best chance.'

'What guarantee have I – '

'That I shall keep faith? The word of Hercule Poirot. You will sign? Good. Hastings, be so kind as to pull that left-hand blind half-way up. That is the signal that Mr Radnor may leave unmolested.'

White, muttering oaths, Radnor hurried from the room. Poirot nodded gently.

'A coward! I always knew it.'

'It seems to me, Poirot, that you've acted in a criminal manner,' I cried angrily. 'You always preach against sentiment. And here you are letting a dangerous criminal escape out of sheer sentimentality.'

'That was not sentiment – that was business,' replied Poirot. 'Do you not see, my friend, that we have no shadow of proof against him? Shall I get up and say to twelve stolid Cornishmen that *I*, Hercule Poirot, *know*? They would laugh at me. The only chance was to frighten him and get a confession that way. Those two loafers that I noticed outside came in very useful. Pull down the blind again, will you, Hastings. Not that there was any reason for raising it. It was part of our *mise en scène*.

'Well, well, we must keep our word. Twenty-four hours, did I say? So much longer for poor Mr Pengelley – and it is not more than he deserves; for mark you, he deceived his wife. I am very strong on the family life, as you know. Ah, well, twenty-four hours – and then? I have great faith in Scotland Yard. They will get him, *mon ami*; they will get him.'

THE ADVENTURE OF JOHNNIE WAVERLY

'You can understand the feelings of a mother,' said Mrs Waverly for perhaps the sixth time.

She looked appealingly at Poirot. My little friend, always sympathetic to motherhood in distress, gesticulated reassuringly.

'But yes, but yes, I comprehend perfectly. Have faith in Papa Poirot.'

'The police –' began Mr Waverly.

His wife waved the interruption aside. 'I won't have anything more to do with the police. We trusted to them and look what happened! But I'd heard so much of M. Poirot and the wonderful things he'd done, that I felt he might possibly be able to help us. A mother's feelings –'

Poirot hastily stemmed the reiteration with an eloquent gesture. Mrs Waverly's emotion was obviously genuine, but it assorted strangely with her shrewd, rather hard type of countenance. When I heard later that she was the daughter of a prominent steel manufacturer who had worked his way up in the world from an office boy to his present eminence, I realized that she had inherited many of the paternal qualities.

Mr Waverly was a big, florid, jovial-looking man. He stood with his legs straddled wide apart and looked the type of the country squire.

'I suppose you know all about this business, M. Poirot?'

The question was almost superfluous. For some days past the papers had been full of the sensational kidnapping of little Johnnie Waverly, the three-year-old son and heir of Marcus Waverly, Esq., of Waverly Court, Surrey, one of the oldest families in England.

'The main facts I know, of course, but recount to me the whole story, monsieur, I beg of you. And in detail if you please.'

'Well, I suppose the beginning of the whole thing was about ten days ago when I got an anonymous letter – beastly things, anyway – that I couldn't make head or tail of. The writer had the impudence to demand that I should pay him twenty-five thousand pounds – twenty-five thousand pounds, M. Poirot! Failing my agreement, he threatened to kidnap Johnnie. Of course I threw the thing into the wastepaper basket without more ado. Thought it was some silly joke. Five days later I got another letter. "Unless you pay, your son will be kidnapped on the twenty-ninth." That was on the twenty-seventh. Ada was worried, but I couldn't bring myself to treat the matter seriously. Damn it all, we're in England. Nobody goes about kidnapping children and holding them up to ransom.'

'It is not a common practice, certainly,' said Poirot. 'Proceed, monsieur.'

'Well, Ada gave me no peace, so – feeling a bit of a fool – I laid the matter before Scotland Yard. They didn't seem to take the thing very seriously – inclined to my view that it was some silly joke. On the twenty-eighth I got a third letter. "You have not paid. Your son will be taken from you at twelve o'clock noon tomorrow, the twenty-ninth. It will cost you fifty thousand pounds to recover him." Up I drove to Scotland Yard again. This time they were more impressed. They inclined to the view that the letters were written by a lunatic, and that in all probability an attempt of some kind would be made at the hour stated. They assured me that they would take all due precautions. Inspector NcNeil and a sufficient force would come down to Waverly on the morrow and take charge.

'I went home much relieved in mind. Yet we already had the feeling of being in a state of siege. I gave orders that no stranger was to be admitted, and that no one was to leave the house. The evening passed off without any untoward incident, but on the following morning my wife was seriously unwell. Alarmed by her condition, I sent for Doctor Dakers. Her symptoms appeared to puzzle him. While hesitating to suggest that she had been poisoned, I could see that that was what was in his mind. There was no danger, he assured me, but it would be a day or two before she would be able to get about again.

Returning to my own room, I was startled and amazed to find a note pinned to my pillow. It was in the same handwriting as the others and contained just three words: "At twelve o'clock".

'I admit, M. Poirot, that then I saw red! Someone in the house was in this – one of the servants. I had them all up, blackguarded them right and left. They never split on each other; it was Miss Collins, my wife's companion, who informed me that she had seen Johnnie's nurse slip down the drive early that morning. I taxed her with it, and she broke down. She had left the child with the nursery maid and stolen out to meet a friend of hers – a man! Pretty goings on! She denied having pinned the note to my pillow – she may have been speaking the truth, I don't know. I felt I couldn't take the risk of the child's own nurse being in the plot. One of the servants was implicated – of that I was sure. Finally I lost my temper and sacked the whole bunch, nurse and all. I gave them an hour to pack their boxes and get out of the house.'

Mr Waverly's face was quite two shades redder as he remembered his just wrath.

'Was not that a little injudicious, monsieur?' suggested Poirot. 'For all you know, you might have been playing into the enemy's hands.'

Mr Waverly stared at him. 'I don't see that. Send the whole lot packing, that was my idea. I wired to London for a fresh lot to be sent down that evening. In the meantime, there'd be only people I could trust in the house: my wife's secretary, Miss Collins, and Tredwell, the butler, who has been with me since I was a boy.'

'And this Miss Collins, how long has she been with you?'

'Just a year,' said Mrs Waverly. 'She has been invaluable to me as a secretary-companion, and is also a very efficient housekeeper.'

'The nurse?'

'She has been with me six months. She came to me with excellent references. All the same, I never really liked her, although Johnnie was quite devoted to her.'

'Still, I gather she had already left when the catastrophe

occurred. Perhaps, Monsieur Waverly, you will be so kind as to continue.'

Mr Waverly resumed his narrative.

'Inspector McNeil arrived about ten-thirty. The servants had all left by then. He declared himself quite satisfied with the internal arrangements. He had various men posted in the park outside, guarding all the approaches to the house, and he assured me that if the whole thing were not a hoax, we should undoubtedly catch my mysterious correspondent.

'I had Johnnie with me, and he and I and the inspector went together into the room we call the council chamber. The inspector locked the door. There is a big grandfather clock there, and as the hands drew near to twelve I don't mind confessing that I was as nervous as a cat. There was a whirring sound, and the clock began to strike. I clutched at Johnnie. I had a feeling a man might drop from the skies. The last stroke sounded, and as it did so, there was a great commotion outside – shouting and running. The inspector flung up the window, and a constable came running up.

'"We've got him sir," he panted. "He was sneaking up through the bushes. He's got a whole dope outfit on him."

'We hurried out on the terrace where two constables were holding a ruffianly-looking fellow in shabby clothes, who was twisting and turning in a vain endeavour to escape. One of the policemen held out an unrolled parcel which they had wrested from their captive. It contained a pad of cotton wool and a bottle of chloroform. It made my blood boil to see it. There was a note, too, addressed to me. I tore it open. It bore the following words: "You should have paid up. To ransom your son will now cost you fifty thousand. In spite of all your precautions he has been abducted on the twenty-ninth as I said."

'I gave a great laugh, the laugh of relief, but as I did so I heard the hum of a motor and a shout. I turned my head. Racing down the drive towards the south lodge at a furious speed was a low, long grey car. It was the man who drove it who shouted, but that was not what gave me a shock of horror. It was the sight of Johnnie's flaxen curls. The child was in the car beside him.

'The inspector ripped out an oath. "The child was here not a minute ago," he cried. His eyes swept over us. We were all there: myself, Tredwell, Miss Collins. "When did you last see him, Mr Waverly?"

'I cast my mind back, trying to remember. When the constable had called us, I had run out with the inspector, forgetting all about Johnnie.

'And then there came a sound that startled us, the chiming of a church clock from the village. With an exclamation the inspector pulled out his watch. It was exactly twelve o'clock. With one common accord we ran to the council chamber; the clock there marked the hour as ten minutes past. Someone must have deliberately tampered with it, for I have never known it gain or lose before. It is a perfect timekeeper.'

Mr Waverly paused. Poirot smiled to himself and straightened a little mat which the anxious father had pushed askew.

'A pleasing little problem, obscure and charming,' murmured Poirot. 'I will investigate it for you with pleasure. Truly it was planned à merveille.'

Mrs Waverly looked at him reproachfully. 'But my boy,' she wailed.

Poirot hastily composed his face and looked the picture of earnest sympathy again. 'He is safe, madame, he is unharmed. Rest assured, these miscreants will take the greatest care of him. Is he not to them the turkey – no, the goose – that lays the golden eggs?'

'M. Poirot, I'm sure there's only one thing to be done – pay up. I was all against it at first – but now! A mother's feelings – '

'But we have interrupted monsieur in his history,' cried Poirot hastily.

'I expect you know the rest pretty well from the papers,' said Mr Waverly. 'Of course, Inspector McNeil got on to the telephone immediately. A description of the car and the man was circulated all round, and it looked at first as though everything was going to turn out all right. A car, answering to the description, with a man and a small boy, had passed through various villages, apparently making for London. At one place they had stopped, and it was noticed that the child was crying and obviously afraid of his companion. When Inspector McNeil announced that the car had been stopped and the man and boy detained, I was almost ill with relief. You know the sequel. The boy was not Johnnie, and the man was an ardent motorist, fond of children, who had picked up a small child playing in the streets of Edenswell, a village about fifteen miles from us, and was kindly giving him a ride. Thanks to the cocksure blundering of the police, all traces have disappeared. Had they not persistently followed the wrong car, they might by now have found the boy.'

'Calm yourself, monsieur. The police are a brave and intelligent force of men. Their mistake was a very natural one. And altogether it was a clever scheme. As to the man they caught in the grounds, I understand that his defence has consisted all along of a persistent denial. He declared that the note and parcel were given to him to deliver at Waverly Court. The man who gave them to him handed him a ten-shilling note and promised him another if it were delivered at exactly ten minutes to twelve. He was to approach the house through the grounds and knock at the side door.'

'I don't believe a word of it,' declared Mrs Waverly hotly. 'It's all a parcel of lies.'

'*En verité*, it is a thin story,' said Poirot reflectively. 'But so far they have not shaken it. I understand, also, that he made a certain accusation?'

His glance interrogated Mr Waverly. The latter got rather red again.

'The fellow had the impertinence to pretend that he recognized in Tredwell the man who gave him the parcel. "Only the bloke has shaved off his moustache." Tredwell, who was born on the estate!'

Poirot smiled a little at the country gentleman's indignation. 'Yet you yourself suspect an inmate of the house to have been accessory to the abduction.'

'Yes, but not Tredwell.'

'And you, madame?' asked Poirot, suddenly turning to her.

'It could not have been Tredwell who gave this tramp the letter and parcel – if anybody ever did, which I don't believe.

It was given him at ten o'clock, he says. At ten o'clock Tredwell was with my husband in the smoking-room.'

'Were you able to see the face of the man in the car, monsieur? Did it resemble that of Tredwell in any way?'

'It was too far away for me to see his face.'

'Has Tredwell a brother, do you know?'

'He had several, but they are all dead. The last one was killed in the war.'

'I am not yet clear as to the grounds of Waverly Court. The car was heading for the south lodge. Is there another entrance?'

'Yes, what we call the east lodge. It can be seen from the other side of the house.'

'It seems to me strange that nobody saw the car entering the grounds.'

'There is a right of way through, and access to a small chapel. A good many cars pass through. The man must have stopped the car in a convenient place and run up to the house just as the alarm was given and attention attracted elsewhere.'

'Unless he was already inside the house,' mused Poirot. 'Is there any place where he could have hidden?'

'Well, we certainly didn't make a thorough search of the house beforehand. There seemed no need. I suppose he might have hidden himself somewhere, but who would have let him in?'

'We shall come to that later. One thing at a time – let us be methodical. There is no special hiding-place in the house? Waverly Court is an old place, and there are sometimes "priests' holes", as they call them.'

'By gad, there *is* a priest's hole. It opens from one of the panels in the hall.'

'Near the council chamber?'

'Just outside the door.'

'*Voilà!*'

'But nobody knows of its existence except my wife and myself.'

'Tredwell?'

'Well – he might have heard of it.'

'Miss Collins?'

57

'I have never mentioned it to her.'

Poirot reflected for a minute.

'Well, monsieur, the next thing is for me to come down to Waverly Court. If I arrive this afternoon, will it suit you?'

'Oh, as soon as possible, please, Monsieur Poirot!' cried Mrs Waverly. 'Read this once more.'

She thrust into his hands the last missive from the enemy which had reached the Waverlys that morning and which had sent her post-haste to Poirot. It gave clever and explicit directions for the paying over of the money, and ended with a threat that the boy's life would pay for any treachery. It was clear that a love of money warred with the essential mother love of Mrs Waverly, and that the latter was at last gaining the day.

Poirot detained Mrs Waverly for a minute behind her husband.

'Madame, the truth, if you please. Do you share your husband's faith in the butler, Tredwell?'

'I have nothing against him, Monsieur Poirot, I cannot see how he can have been concerned in this, but – well, I have never liked him – never!'

'One other thing, madame, can you give me the address of the child's nurse?'

'149 Netherall Road, Hammersmith. You don't imagine – '

'Never do I imagine. Only – I employ the little grey cells. And sometimes, just sometimes, I have a little idea.'

Poirot came back to me as the door closed.

'So madame has never liked the butler. It is interesting, that, eh, Hastings?'

I refused to be drawn. Poirot has deceived me so often that I now go warily. There is always a catch somewhere.

After completing an elaborate outdoor toilet, we set off for Netherall Road. We were fortunate enough to find Miss Jessie Withers at home. She was a pleasant-faced woman of thirty-five, capable and superior. I could not believe that she could be mixed up in the affair. She was bitterly resentful of the way she had been dismissed, but admitted that she had been in the wrong. She was engaged to be married to a painter and decorator who happened to be in the neighbourhood, and she had run out to meet him. The thing seemed natural enough. I could not quite understand Poirot. All his questions seemed to me quite irrelevant. They were concerned mainly with the daily routine of her life at Waverly Court. I was frankly bored and glad when Poirot took his departure.

'Kidnapping is an easy job, *mon ami*,' he observed, as he hailed a taxi in the Hammersmith Road and ordered it to drive to Waterloo. 'That child could have been abducted with the greatest ease any day for the last three years.'

'I don't see that that advances us much,' I remarked coldly.

'*Au contraire*, it advances us enormously, but enormously! If you must wear a tie pin, Hastings, at least let it be in the exact centre of your tie. At present it is at least a sixteenth of an inch too much to the right.'

Waverly Court was a fine old place and had recently been restored with taste and care. Mr Waverly showed us the council chamber, the terrace, and all the various spots connected with the case. Finally, at Poirot's request, he pressed a spring in the wall, a panel slid aside, and a short passage led us into the priest's hole.

'You see,' said Waverly. 'There is nothing here.'

The tiny room was bare enough, there was not even the mark of a footstep on the floor. I joined Poirot where he was bending attentively over a mark in the corner.

'What do you make of this, my friend?'

There were four imprints close together.

'A dog,' I cried.

'A very small dog, Hastings.'

'A Pom.'

'Smaller than a Pom.'

'A griffon?' I suggested doubtfully.

'Smaller even than a griffon. A species unknown to the Kennel Club.'

I looked at him. His face was alight with excitement and satisfaction.

'I was right,' he murmured. 'I knew I was right. Come, Hastings.'

As we stepped out into the hall and the panel closed behind

us, a young lady came out of a door farther down the passage. Mr Waverly presented her to us.

'Miss Collins.'

Miss Collins was about thirty years of age, brisk and alert in manner. She had fair, rather dull hair, and wore pince-nez.

At Poirot's request, we passed into a small morning-room, and he questioned her closely as to the servants and particularly as to Tredwell. She admitted that she did not like the butler.

'He gives himself airs,' she explained.

They then went into the question of the food eaten by Mrs Waverly on the night of the 28th. Miss Collins declared that she had partaken of the same dishes upstairs in her sitting-room and had felt no ill effects. As she was departing I nudged Poirot.

'The dog,' I whispered.

'Ah, yes, the dog!' He smiled broadly. 'Is there a dog kept here by any chance, mademoiselle?'

'There are two retrievers in the kennels outside.'

'No, I mean a small dog, a toy dog.'

'No – nothing of the kind.'

Poirot permitted her to depart. Then, pressing the bell, he remarked to me, 'She lies, that Mademoiselle Collins. Possibly I should, also, in her place. Now for the butler.'

Tredwell was a dignified individual. He told his story with perfect aplomb, and it was essentially the same as that of Mr Waverly. He admitted that he knew the secret of the priest's hole.

When he finally withdrew, pontifical to the last, I met Poirot's quizzical eyes.

'What do you make of it all, Hastings?'

'What do you?' I parried.

'How cautious you become. Never, never will the grey cells function unless you stimulate them. Ah, but I will not tease you! Let us make our deductions together. What points strike us specially as being difficult?'

'There is one thing that strikes me,' I said. 'Why did the man who kidnapped the child go out by the south lodge instead of by the east lodge where no one would see him?'

'That is a very good point, Hastings, an excellent one. I will match it with another. Why warn the Waverlys beforehand? Why not simply kidnap the child and hold him to ransom?'

'Because they hoped to get the money without being forced to action.'

'Surely it was very unlikely that the money would be paid on a mere threat?'

'Also they wanted to focus attention on twelve o'clock, so that when the tramp man was seized, the other could emerge from his hiding-place and get away with the child unnoticed.'

'That does not alter the fact that they were making a thing difficult that was perfectly easy. If they do not specify a time or date, nothing would be easier than to wait their chance, and carry off the child in a motor one day when he is out with his nurse.'

'Ye – es,' I admitted doubtfully.

'In fact, there is a deliberate playing of the farce! Now let us approach the question from another side. Everything goes to show that there was an accomplice inside the house. Point number one, the mysterious poisoning of Mrs Waverly. Point number two, the letter pinned to the pillow. Point number three, the putting on of the clock ten minutes – all inside jobs. And an additional fact that you may not have noticed. There was no dust in the priest's hole. It had been swept out with a broom.

'Now then, we have four people in the house. We can exclude the nurse, since she could not have swept out the priest's hole, though she could have attended to the other three points. Four people, Mr and Mrs Waverly, Tredwell, the butler, and Miss Collins. We will take Miss Collins first. We have nothing much against her, except that we know very little about her, that she is obviously an intelligent young woman, and that she has only been here a year.'

'She lied about the dog, you said,' I reminded him.

'Ah, yes, the dog.' Poirot gave a peculiar smile. 'Now let us pass to Tredwell. There are several suspicious facts against him. For one thing, the tramp declares that it was Tredwell who gave him the parcel in the village.'

'But Tredwell can prove an alibi on that point.'

'Even then, he could have poisoned Mrs Waverly, pinned the note to the pillow, put on the clock, and swept out the priest's hole. On the other hand, he has been born and bred in the service of the Waverlys. It seems unlikely in the last degree that he should connive at the abduction of the son of the house. It is not in the picture!'

'Well, then?'

'We must proceed logically – however absurd it may seem. We will briefly consider Mrs Waverly. But she is rich, the money is hers. It is her money which has restored this impoverished estate. There would be no reason for her to kidnap her son and pay over her money to herself. The husband, no, is in a different position. He has a rich wife. It is not the same thing as being rich himself – in fact I have a little idea that the lady is not very fond of parting with her money, except on a very good pretext. But Mr Waverly, you can see at once, he is a *bon viveur*.'

'Impossible,' I spluttered.

'Not at all. Who sends away the servants? Mr Waverly. He can write the notes, drug his wife, put on the hands of the clock, and establish an excellent alibi for his faithful retainer Tredwell. Tredwell has never liked Mrs Waverly. He is devoted to his master and is willing to obey his orders implicitly. There were three of them in it. Waverly, Tredwell, and some friend of Waverly. That is the mistake the police made, they made no further inquiries about the man who drove the grey car with the wrong child in it. He was the third man. He picks up a child in a village near by, a boy with flaxen curls. He drives in through the east lodge and passes out through the south lodge just at the right moment, waving his hand and shouting. They cannot see his face or the number of the car, so obviously they cannot see the child's face, either. Then he lays a false trail to London. In the meantime, Tredwell has done his part in arranging for the parcel and note to be delivered by a rough-looking gentleman. His master can provide an alibi in the unlikely case of the man recognizing him, in spite of the false moustache he wore. As for Mr Waverly, as soon as the hullabaloo occurs outside, and the inspector rushes out, he quickly hides the child in the priest's hole, follows him out. Later in the day, when the inspector is gone and Miss Collins is out of the way, it will be easy enough to drive him off to some safe place in his own car.'

'But what about the dog?' I asked. 'And Miss Collins lying?'

'That was my little joke. I asked her if there were any toy dogs in the house, and she said no – but doubtless there are some – in the nursery! You see, Mr Waverly placed some toys in the priest's hole to keep Johnnie amused and quiet.'

'M. Poirot – ' Mr Waverly entered the room – 'have you discovered anything? Have you any clue to where the boy has been taken?'

Poirot handed him a piece of paper. 'Here is the address.'

'But this is a blank sheet.'

'Because I am waiting for you to write it down for me.'

'What the – ' Mr Waverly's face turned purple.

'I know everything, monsieur. I give you twenty-four hours to return the boy. Your ingenuity will be equal to the task of explaining his reappearance. Otherwise, Mrs Waverly will be informed of the exact sequence of events.'

Mr Waverly sank down in a chair and buried his face in his hands. 'He is with my old nurse, ten miles away. He is happy and well cared for.'

'I have no doubt of that. If I did not believe you to be a good father at heart, I should not be willing to give you another chance.'

'The scandal – '

'Exactly. Your name is an old and honoured one. Do not jeopardize it again. Good evening, Mr Waverly. Ah, by the way, one word of advice. Always sweep in the corners!'

'But above everything – no publicity,' said Mr Marcus Hardman for perhaps the fourteenth time.

The word *publicity* occurred throughout his conversation with the regularity of a leitmotif. Mr Hardman was a small man, delicately plump, with exquisitely manicured hands and a plaintive tenor voice. In his way, he was somewhat of a celebrity and the fashionable life was his profession. He was rich, but not remarkably so, and he spent his money zealously in the pursuit of social pleasure. His hobby was collecting. He had the collector's soul. Old lace, old fans, antique jewellery – nothing crude or modern for Marcus Hardman.

Poirot and I, obeying an urgent summons, had arrived to find the little man writhing in an agony of indecision. Under the circumstances, to call in the police was abhorrent to him. On the other hand, not to call them in was to acquiesce in the loss of some of the gems of his collection. He hit upon Poirot as a compromise.

'My rubies, Monsieur Poirot, and the emerald necklace said to have belonged to Catherine de' Medici. Oh, the emerald necklace!'

'If you will recount to me the circumstances of their disappearance?' suggested Poirot gently.

'I am endeavouring to do so. Yesterday afternoon I had a little tea party – quite an informal affair, some half a dozen people or so. I have given one or two of them during the season, and though perhaps I should not say so, they have been quite a success. Some good music – Nacora, the pianist, and Katherine Bird, the Australian contralto – in the big studio. Well, early in the afternoon, I was showing my guests my collection of medieval jewels. I keep them in the small wall safe over there. It is arranged like a cabinet inside, with coloured velvet background, to display the stones. Afterwards we inspected the fans – in the case on the wall. Then we all went to the studio for music. It was not until after everyone had gone that I discovered the safe rifled! I must have failed to shut it properly, and someone had seized the opportunity to denude it of its contents. The rubies, Monsieur Poirot, the emerald necklace – the collection of a lifetime! What would I not give to recover them! But there must be no publicity! You fully understand that, do you not, Monsieur Poirot? My own guests, my personal friends! It would be a horrible scandal!'

'Who was the last person to leave this room when you went to the studio?'

'Mr Johnston. You may know him? The South African millionaire. He has just rented the Abbotburys' house in Park Lane. He lingered behind a few moments, I remember. But surely, oh, surely it could not be he!'

'Did any of your guests return to this room during the afternoon on any pretext?'

'I was prepared for that question, Monsieur Poirot. Three of them did so. Countess Vera Rossakoff, Mr Bernard Parker, and Lady Runcorn.'

'Let us hear about them.'

'The Countess Rossakoff is a very charming Russian lady, a member of the old régime. She has recently come to this country. She had bade me goodbye, and I was therefore somewhat surprised to find her in this room apparently gazing in rapture at my cabinet of fans. You know, Monsieur Poirot, the more I think of it, the more suspicious it seems to me. Don't you agree?'

'Extremely suspicious; but let us hear about the others.'

'Well, Parker simply came here to fetch a case of miniatures that I was anxious to show to Lady Runcorn.'

'And Lady Runcorn herself?'

'As I dare say you know, Lady Runcorn is a middle-aged woman of considerable force of character who devotes most of her time to various charitable committees. She simply returned to fetch a handbag she had laid down somewhere.'

'*Bien*, monsieur. So we have four possible suspects. The Russian countess, the English *grande dame*, the South African millionaire, and Mr Bernard Parker. Who *is* Mr Parker, by the way?'

The question appeared to embarrass Mr Hardman considerably.

'He is – er – he is a young fellow. Well, in fact, a young fellow I know.'

'I had already deduced as much,' replied Poirot gravely. 'What does he do, this Mr Parker?'

'He is a young man about town – not, perhaps, quite in the swim, if I may so express myself.'

'How did he come to be a friend of yours, may I ask?'

'Well – er – on one or two occasions he has – performed certain little commissions for me.'

'Continue, monsieur,' said Poirot.

Hardman looked piteously at him. Evidently the last thing he wanted to do was to continue. But as Poirot maintained an inexorable silence, he capitulated.

'You see, Monsieur Poirot – it is well known that I am interested in antique jewels. Sometimes there is a family heirloom to be disposed of – which, mind you, would never be sold in the open market or to a dealer. But a private sale to me is a very different matter. Parker arranges the details of such things, he is in touch with both sides, and thus any little embarrassment is avoided. He brings anything of that kind to my notice. For instance, the Countess Rossakoff has brought some family jewels with her from Russia. She is anxious to sell them. Bernard Parker was to have arranged the transaction.'

'I see,' said Poirot thoughtfully. 'And you trust him implicitly?'

'I have had no reason to do otherwise.'

'Mr Hardman, of these four people, which do you yourself suspect?'

'Oh, Monsieur Poirot, what a question! They are my friends, as I told you. I suspect none of them – or all of them, whichever way you like to put it.'

'I do not agree. You suspect one of those four. It is not Countess Rossakoff. It is not Mr Parker. Is it Lady Runcorn or Mr Johnston?'

'You drive me into a corner, Monsieur Poirot, you do indeed. I am most anxious to have no scandal. Lady Runcorn belongs to one of the oldest families in England; but it is true, it is most unfortunately true, that her aunt, Lady Caroline, suffered from a most melancholy affliction. It was understood, of course, by all her friends, and her maid returned the teaspoons, or whatever it was, as promptly as possible. You see my predicament!'

'So Lady Runcorn had an aunt who was a kleptomaniac? Very interesting. You permit that I examine the safe?'

Mr Hardman assenting, Poirot pushed back the door of the safe and examined the interior. The empty velvet-lined shelves gaped at us.

'Even now the door does not shut properly,' murmured Poirot, as he swung it to and fro. 'I wonder why? Ah, what have we here? A glove, caught in the hinge. A man's glove.'

He held it out to Mr Hardman.

'That's not one of my gloves,' the latter declared.

'Aha! Something more!' Poirot bent deftly and picked up a small object from the floor of the safe. It was a flat cigarette case made of black moiré.

'My cigarette case!' cried Mr Hardman.

'Yours? Surely not, monsieur. Those are not your initials.'

He pointed to an entwined monogram of two letters executed in platinum.

Hardman took it in his hand.

'You are right,' he declared. 'It is very like mine, but the initials are different. A "B" and a "P". Good heavens – Parker!'

'It would seem so,' said Poirot. 'A somewhat careless young man – especially if the glove is his also. That would be a double clue, would it not?'

'Bernard Parker!' murmured Hardman. 'What a relief! Well, Monsieur Poirot, I leave it to you to recover the jewels. Place the matter in the hands of the police if you think fit – that is, if you are quite sure that it is he who is guilty.'

'See you, my friend,' said Poirot to me, as we left the house together, 'he has one law for the titled, and another law for the

67

plain, this Mr Hardman. Me, I have not yet been ennobled, so I am on the side of the plain. I have sympathy for this young man. The whole thing was a little curious, was it not? There was Hardman suspecting Lady Runcorn; there was I, suspecting the Countess and Johnston; and all the time, the obscure Mr Parker was our man.'

'Why did you suspect the other two?'

'*Parbleu*! It is such a simple thing to be a Russian refugee or a South African millionaire. Any woman can call herself a Russian countess; anyone can buy a house in Park Lane and call himself a South African millionaire. Who is going to contradict them? But I observe that we are passing through Bury Street. Our careless young friend lives here. Let us, as you say, strike while the iron is in the fire.'

Mr Bernard Parker was at home. We found him reclining on some cushions, clad in an amazing dressing-gown of purple and orange. I have seldom taken a greater dislike to anyone than I did to this particular young man with his white, effeminate face and affected lisping speech.

'Good morning, monsieur,' said Poirot briskly. 'I come from Mr Hardman. Yesterday, at the party, somebody has stolen all his jewels. Permit me to ask you, monsieur – is this your glove?'

Mr Parker's mental processes did not seem very rapid. He stared at the glove, as though gathering his wits together.

'Where did you find it?' he asked at last.

'Is it your glove, monsieur?'

Mr Parker appeared to make up his mind.

'No, it isn't,' he declared.

'And this cigarette case, is that yours?'

'Certainly not. I always carry a silver one.'

'Very well, monsieur. I go to put matters in the hands of the police.'

'Oh, I say, I wouldn't do that if I were you,' cried Mr Parker in some concern. 'Beastly unsympathetic people, the police. Wait a bit. I'll go round and see old Hardman. Look here – oh, stop a minute.'

But Poirot beat a determined retreat.

'We have given him something to think about, have we not?' he chuckled. 'Tomorrow we will observe what has occurred.'

But we were destined to have a reminder of the Hardman case that afternoon. Without the least warning the door flew open, and a whirlwind in human form invaded our privacy, bringing with her a swirl of sables (it was as cold as only an English June day can be) and a hat rampant with slaughtered ospreys. Countess Vera Rossakoff was a somewhat disturbing personality.

'You are Monsieur Poirot? What is this that you have done? You accuse that poor boy! It is infamous. It is scandalous. I know him. He is a chicken, a lamb – never would he steal. He has done everything for me. Will I stand by and see him martyred and butchered?'

'Tell me, madame, is this his cigarette case?' Poirot held out the black moiré case.

The Countess paused for a moment while she inspected it.

'Yes, it is his. I know it well. What of it? Did you find it in the room? We were all there; he dropped it then, I suppose. Ah, you policemen, you are worse than the Red Guards – '

'And is this his glove?'

'How should I know? One glove is like another. Do not try to stop me – he must be set free. His character must be cleared. You shall do it. I will sell my jewels and give you much money.'

'Madame – '

'It is agreed, then? No, no, do not argue. The poor boy! He came to me, the tears in his eyes. "I will save you," I said. "I will go to this man – this ogre, this monster! Leave it to Vera." Now it is settled, I go.'

With as little ceremony as she had come, she swept from the room, leaving an overpowering perfume of an exotic nature behind her.

'What a woman!' I exclaimed. 'And what furs!'

'Ah, yes, *they* were genuine enough. Could a spurious countess have real furs? My little joke, Hastings ... No, she is truly Russian, I fancy. Well, well, so Master Bernard went bleating to her.'

'The cigarette case is his. I wonder if the glove is also – '

With a smile Poirot drew from his pocket a second glove and placed it by the first. There was no doubt of their being a pair.

'Where did you get the second one, Poirot?'

'It was thrown down with a stick on the table in the hall in Bury Street. Truly, a very careless young man, Monsieur Parker. Well, well, *mon ami* – we must be thorough. Just for the form of the thing, I will make a little visit to Park Lane.'

Needless to say, I accompanied my friend. Johnston was out, but we saw his private secretary. It transpired that Johnston had only recently arrived from South Africa. He had never been in England before.

'He is interested in precious stones, is he not?' hazarded Poirot.

'Gold mining is nearer the mark,' laughed the secretary.

Poirot came away from the interview thoughtful. Late that evening, to my utter surprise, I found him earnestly studying a Russian grammar.

'Good heavens, Poirot!' I cried. 'Are you learning Russian in order to converse with the Countess in her own language?'

'She certainly would not listen to my English, my friend!'

'But surely, Poirot, well-born Russians invariably speak French?'

'You are a mine of information, Hastings! I will cease puzzling over the intricacies of the Russian alphabet.'

He threw the book from him with a dramatic gesture. I was not entirely satisfied. There was a twinkle in his eye which I knew of old. It was an invariable sign that Hercule Poirot was pleased with himself.

'Perhaps,' I said sapiently, 'you doubt her being really a Russian. You are going to test her?'

'Ah, no, no, she is Russian all right.'

'Well, then – '

'If you really want to distinguish yourself over this case, Hastings, I recommend *First Steps in Russian* as an invaluable aid.'

Then he laughed and would say no more. I picked up the book from the floor and dipped into it curiously, but could make neither head nor tail of Poirot's remarks.

The following morning brought us no news of any kind, but that did not seem to worry my little friend. At breakfast, he announced his intention of calling upon Mr Hardman early in the day. We found the elderly social butterfly at home, and seemingly a little calmer than on the previous day.

'Well, Monsieur Poirot, any news?' he demanded eagerly.

Poirot handed him a slip of paper.

'That is the person who took the jewels, monsieur. Shall I put matters in the hands of the police? Or would you prefer me to recover the jewels without bringing the police into the matter?'

Mr Hardman was staring at the paper. At last he found his voice.

'Most astonishing. I should infinitely prefer to have no scandal in the matter. I give you *carte blanche*, Monsieur Poirot. I am sure you will be discreet.'

Our next procedure was to hail a taxi, which Poirot ordered to drive to the Carlton. There he inquired for Countess Rossakoff. In a few minutes we were ushered up into the lady's suite. She came to meet us with outstretched hands, arrayed in a marvellous negligée of barbaric design.

'Monsieur Poirot!' she cried. 'You have succeeded? You have cleared that poor infant?'

'Madame la Comtesse, your friend Mr Parker is perfectly safe from arrest.'

'Ah, but you are the clever little man! Superb! And so quickly too.'

'On the other hand, I have promised Mr Hardman that the jewels shall be returned to him today.'

'So?'

'Therefore, madame, I should be extremely obliged if you would place them in my hands without delay. I am sorry to hurry you, but I am keeping a taxi – in case it should be necessary for me to go on to Scotland Yard; and we Belgians, madame, we practise the thrift.'

The Countess had lighted a cigarette. For some seconds she sat perfectly still, blowing smoke rings, and gazing steadily at Poirot. Then she burst into a laugh, and rose. She went across to the bureau, opened a drawer, and took out a black silk handbag. She tossed it lightly to Poirot. Her tone, when she spoke, was perfectly light and unmoved.

'We Russians, on the contrary, practise prodigality,' she said. 'And to do that, unfortunately, one must have money. You need not look inside. They are all there.'

Poirot arose.

'I congratulate you, madame, on your quick intelligence and your promptitude.'

'Ah! But since you were keeping your taxi waiting, what else could I do?'

'You are too amiable, madame. You are remaining long in London?'

'I am afraid no – owing to you.'

'Accept my apologies.'

'We shall meet again elsewhere, perhaps.'

'I hope so.'

'And I – do not!' exclaimed the Countess with a laugh. 'It is a great compliment that I pay you there – there are very few men in the world whom I fear. Goodbye, Monsieur Poirot.'

'Goodbye, Madame la Comtesse. Ah – pardon me, I forgot! Allow me to return you your cigarette case.'

And with a bow he handed to her the little black moiré case we had found in the safe. She accepted it without any change of expression – just a lifted eyebrow and a murmured: 'I see!'

'What a woman!' cried Poirot enthusiastically as we descended the stairs. '*Mon Dieu, quelle femme!* Not a word of argument – of protestation, of bluff! One quick glance, and she had sized up the position correctly. I tell you, Hastings, a woman who can accept defeat like that – with a careless smile – will go far! She is dangerous, she has the nerves of steel; she – ' He tripped heavily.

'If you can manage to moderate your transports and look where you're going, it might be as well,' I suggested. 'When did you first suspect the Countess?'

'*Mon ami*, it was the glove *and* the cigarette case – the double clue, shall we say – that worried me. Bernard Parker might easily have dropped one or the other – but hardly both. Ah, no, that would have been *too* careless! In the same way, if someone else had placed them there to incriminate Parker, one would have been sufficient – the cigarette case *or* the glove – again not both. So I was forced to the conclusion that one of the two things did *not* belong to Parker. I imagined at first that the case was his, and that the glove was not. But when I discovered the fellow to the glove, I saw that it was the other way about. Whose, then, was the cigarette case? Clearly, it could not belong to Lady Runcorn. The initials were wrong. Mr Johnston? Only if he were here under a false name. I interviewed his secretary, and it was apparent at once that everything was clear and above board. There was no reticence about Mr Johnston's past. The Countess, then? She was supposed to have brought jewels with her from Russia; she had only to take the stones from their settings, and it was extremely doubtful if they could ever be identified. What could be easier for her than to pick up one of Parker's gloves from the hall that day and thrust it into the safe? But, *bien sûr*, she did not intend to drop her own cigarette case.'

'But if the case was hers, why did it have "*B.P.*" on it? The Countess's initials are *V.R.*'

Poirot smiled gently upon me.

'Exactly, *mon ami*; but in the Russian alphabet, *B* is *V* and *P* is *R*.'

'Well, you couldn't expect me to guess that. I don't know Russian.'

'Neither do I, Hastings. That is why I bought my little book – and urged it on your attention.'

He sighed.

'A remarkable woman. I have a feeling, my friend – a very decided feeling – I shall meet her again. Where, I wonder?'

'After all, there's nothing like the country, is there?' said Inspector Japp, breathing in heavily through his nose and out through his mouth in the most approved fashion.

Poirot and I applauded the sentiment heartily. It had been the Scotland Yard inspector's idea that we should all go for the weekend to the little country town of Market Basing. When off duty, Japp was an ardent botanist, and discoursed upon minute flowers possessed of unbelievably lengthy Latin names (somewhat strangely pronounced) with an enthusiasm even greater than that he gave to his cases.

'Nobody knows us, and we know nobody,' explained Japp. 'That's the idea.'

This was not to prove quite the case, however, for the local constable happened to have been transferred from a village fifteen miles away where a case of arsenical poisoning had brought him into contact with the Scotland Yard man. However, his delighted recognition of the great man only enhanced Japp's sense of well-being, and as we sat down to breakfast on Sunday morning in the parlour of the village inn, with the sun shining, and tendrils of honeysuckle thrusting themselves in at the window, we were all in the best of spirits. The bacon and eggs were excellent, the coffee not so good, but passable and boiling hot.

'This is the life,' said Japp. 'When I retire, I shall have a little place in the country. Far from crime, like this!'

'*Le crime, il est partout,*' remarked Poirot, helping himself to a neat square of bread, and frowning at a sparrow which had balanced itself impertinently on the windowsill.

I quoted lightly:

> 'That rabbit has a pleasant face,
> His private life is a disgrace

I really could not tell to you
The awful things that rabbits do.'

'Lord,' said Japp, stretching himself backward, 'I believe I could manage another egg, and perhaps a rasher or two of bacon. What do you say, Captain?'

'I'm with you,' I returned heartily. 'What about you, Poirot?'

Poirot shook his head.

'One must not so replenish the stomach that the brain refuses to function,' he remarked.

'I'll risk replenishing the stomach a bit more,' laughed Japp. 'I take a large size in stomachs; and by the way, you're getting stout yourself, M. Poirot. Here, miss, eggs and bacon twice.'

At that moment, however, an imposing form blocked the doorway. It was Constable Pollard.

'I hope you'll excuse me troubling the inspector, gentlemen, but I'd be glad of his advice.'

'I'm on holiday,' said Japp hastily. 'No work for me. What is the case?'

'Gentleman up at Leigh House – shot himself – through the head.'

'Well, they will do it,' said Japp prosaically. 'Debt, or a woman, I suppose. Sorry I can't help you, Pollard.'

'The point is,' said the constable, 'that he can't have shot himself. Leastways, that's what Dr Giles says.'

Japp put down his cup.

'*Can't* have shot himself? What do you mean?'

'That's what Dr Giles says,' repeated Pollard. 'He says it's plumb impossible. He's puzzled to death, the door being locked on the inside and the windows bolted; but he sticks to it that the man couldn't have committed suicide.'

That settled it. The further supply of bacon and eggs was waved aside, and a few minutes later we were all walking as fast as we could in the direction of Leigh House, Japp eagerly questioning the constable.

The name of the deceased was Walter Protheroe; he was a

man of middle age and something of a recluse. He had come to Market Basing eight years ago and rented Leigh House, a rambling, dilapidated old mansion fast falling into ruin. He lived in a corner of it, his wants attended to by a housekeeper whom he had brought with him. Miss Clegg was her name, and she was a very superior woman and highly thought of in the village. Just lately Mr Protheroe had had visitors staying with him, a Mr and Mrs Parker from London. This morning, unable to get a reply when she went to call her master, and finding the door locked, Miss Clegg became alarmed, and telephoned for the police and the doctor. Constable Pollard and Dr Giles had arrived at the same moment. Their united efforts had succeeded in breaking down the oak door of his bedroom.

Mr Protheroe was lying on the floor, shot through the head, and the pistol was clasped in his right hand. It looked a clear case of suicide.

After examining the body, however, Dr Giles became clearly perplexed, and finally he drew the constable aside, and communicated his perplexities to him; whereupon Pollard had at once thought of Japp. Leaving the doctor in charge, he had hurried down to the inn.

By the time the constable's recital was over, we had arrived at Leigh House, a big, desolate house surrounded by an unkempt, weed-ridden garden. The front door was open, and we passed at once into the hall and from there into a small morning-room whence proceeded the sound of voices. Four people were in the room: a somewhat flashily dressed man with a shifty, unpleasant face to whom I took an immediate dislike; a woman of much the same type, though handsome in a coarse fashion; another woman dressed in neat black who stood apart from the rest, and whom I took to be the housekeeper; and a tall man dressed in sporting tweeds, with a clever, capable face, and who was clearly in command of the situation.

'Dr Giles,' said the constable, 'this is Detective-Inspector Japp of Scotland Yard, and his two friends.'

The doctor greeted us and made us known to Mr and Mrs Parker. Then we accompanied them upstairs. Pollard, in obedience to a sign from Japp, remained below, as it were on guard over the household. The doctor led us upstairs and along a passage. A door was open at the end; splinters hung from the hinges, and the door itself had crashed to the floor inside the room.

We went in. The body was still lying on the floor. Mr Protheroe had been a man of middle age, bearded, with hair grey at the temples. Japp went and knelt by the body.

'Why couldn't you leave it as you found it?' he grumbled.

The doctor shrugged his shoulders.

'We thought it a clear case of suicide.'

'H'm!' said Japp. 'Bullet entered the head behind the left ear.'

'Exactly,' said the doctor. 'Clearly impossible for him to have fired it himself. He'd have had to twist his hand right round his head. It couldn't have been done.'

'Yet you found the pistol clasped in his hand? Where is it, by the way?'

The doctor nodded to the table.

'But it wasn't clasped in his hand,' he said. 'It was inside the hand, but the fingers weren't closed over it.'

'Put there afterwards,' said Japp; 'that's clear enough.' He was examining the weapon. 'One cartridge fired. We'll test it for fingerprints, but I doubt if we'll find any but yours, Dr Giles. How long has he been dead?'

'Some time last night. I can't give the time to an hour or so, as those wonderful doctors in detective stories do. Roughly, he's been dead about twelve hours.'

So far, Poirot had not made a move of any kind. He had remained by my side, watching Japp at work and listening to his questions. Only, from time to time, he had sniffed the air very delicately, and as if puzzled. I too had sniffed, but could detect nothing to arouse interest. The air seemed perfectly fresh and devoid of odour. And yet, from time to time, Poirot continued to sniff it dubiously, as though his keener nose detected something I had missed.

Now, as Japp moved away from the body, Poirot knelt down by it. He took no interest in the wound. I thought at first that he was examining the fingers of the hand that had held the pistol, but in a minute I saw that it was a handkerchief carried in the coat-sleeve that interested him. Mr Protheroe was dressed in a dark grey lounge-suit. Finally Poirot got up from his knees, but his eyes still strayed back to the handkerchief as though puzzled.

Japp called to him to come and help to lift the door. Seizing my opportunity, I too knelt down, and taking the handkerchief from the sleeve, scrutinized it minutely. It was a perfectly plain handkerchief of white cambric; there was no mark or stain on it of any kind. I replaced it, shaking my head and confessing myself baffled.

The others had raised the door. I realized that they were hunting for the key. They looked in vain.

'That settles it,' said Japp. 'The window's shut and bolted. The murderer left by the door, locking it and taking the key with him. He thought it would be accepted that Protheroe had locked himself in and shot himself, and that the absence of the key would not be noticed. You agree, M. Poirot?'

'I agree, yes; but it would have been simpler and better to slip the key back inside the room under the door. Then it would look as though it had fallen from the lock.'

'Ah, well, you can't expect everybody to have the bright ideas that you have. You'd have been a holy terror if you'd taken to crime. Any remarks to make, M. Poirot?'

Poirot, it seemed to me, was somewhat at a loss. He looked round the room and remarked mildly and almost apologetically: 'He smoked a lot, this monsieur.'

True enough, the grate was filled with cigarette-stubs, as was an ashtray that stood on a small table near the big armchair.

'He must have got through about twenty cigarettes last night,' remarked Japp. Stooping down, he examined the contents of the grate carefully, then transferred his attention to the ashtray. 'They're all the same kind,' he announced, 'and smoked by the same man. There's nothing there, M. Poirot.'

'I did not suggest that there was,' murmured my friend.

'Ha,' cried Japp, 'what's this?' He pounced on something bright and glittering that lay on the floor near the dead man. 'A broken cuff-link. I wonder who this belongs to. Dr Giles, I'd be obliged if you'd go down and send up the housekeeper.'

'What about the Parkers? He's very anxious to leave the house – says he's got urgent business in London.'

'I dare say. It'll have to get on without him. By the way things are going, it's likely that there'll be some urgent business down here for him to attend to! Send up the housekeeper, and don't let either of the Parkers give you and Pollard the slip. Did any of the household come in here this morning?'

The doctor reflected.

'No, they stood outside in the corridor while Pollard and I came in.'

'Sure of that?'

'Absolutely certain.'

The doctor departed on his mission.

'Good man, that,' said Japp approvingly. 'Some of these sporting doctors are first-class fellows. Well, I wonder who shot this chap. It looks like one of the three in the house. I hardly suspect the housekeeper. She's had eight years to shoot him in if she wanted to. I wonder who these Parkers are? They're not a prepossessing-looking couple.'

Miss Clegg appeared at this juncture. She was a thin, gaunt woman with neat grey hair parted in the middle, very staid and calm in manner. Nevertheless there was an air of efficiency about her which commanded respect. In answer to Japp's questions, she explained that she had been with the dead man for fourteen years. He had been a generous and considerate master. She had never seen Mr and Mrs Parker until three days ago, when they arrived unexpectedly to stay. She was of the opinion that they had asked themselves – the master had certainly not seemed pleased to see them. The cuff-links which Japp showed her had not belonged to Mr Protheroe – she was sure of that. Questioned about the pistol, she said that she believed her master had a weapon of that kind. He kept it locked up. She had seen it once some years ago, but could not say whether this was the same one. She had heard no shot last night, but that was not surprising, as it was a big, rambling house, and her rooms and those prepared for the Parkers were

79

at the other end of the building. She did not know what time Mr Protheroe had gone to bed – he was still up when she retired at half past nine. It was not his habit to go at once to bed when he went to his room. Usually he would sit up half the night, reading and smoking. He was a great smoker.

Then Poirot interposed a question:

'Did your master sleep with his window open or shut, as a rule?'

Miss Clegg considered.

'It was usually open, at any rate at the top.'

'Yet now it is closed. Can you explain that?'

'No, unless he felt a draught and shut it.'

Japp asked her a few more questions and then dismissed her. Next he interviewed the Parkers separately. Mrs Parker was inclined to be hysterical and tearful; Mr Parker was full of bluster and abuse. He denied that the cuff-link was his, but as his wife had previously recognized it, this hardly improved matters for him; and as he had also denied ever having been in Protheroe's room, Japp considered that he had sufficient evidence to apply for a warrant.

Leaving Pollard in charge, Japp bustled back to the village and got into telephonic communication with headquarters. Poirot and I strolled back to the inn.

'You're unusually quiet,' I said. 'Doesn't the case interest you?'

'*Au contraire*, it interests me enormously. But it puzzles me also.'

'The motive is obscure,' I said thoughtfully, 'but I'm certain that Parker's a bad lot. The case against him seems pretty clear but for the lack of motive, and that may come out later.'

'Nothing struck you as being especially significant, although overlooked by Japp?'

I looked at him curiously.

'What have you got up your sleeve, Poirot?'

'What did the dead man have up his sleeve?'

'Oh, that handkerchief!'

'Exactly, that handkerchief.'

'A sailor carries his handkerchief in his sleeve,' I said thoughtfully.

'An excellent point, Hastings, though not the one I had in mind.'

'Anything else?'

'Yes, over and over again I go back to the smell of cigarette-smoke.'

'I didn't smell any,' I cried wonderingly.

'No more did I, *cher ami*.'

I looked earnestly at him. It is so difficult to know when Poirot is pulling one's leg, but he seemed thoroughly in earnest and was frowning to himself.

The inquest took place two days later. In the meantime other evidence had come to light. A tramp had admitted that he had climbed over the wall into the Leigh House garden, where he often slept in a shed that was left unlocked. He declared that at twelve o'clock he had heard two men quarrelling loudly in a room on the first floor. One was demanding a sum of money; the other was angrily refusing. Concealed behind a bush, he had seen the two men as they passed and repassed the lighted window. One he knew well as being Mr Protheroe, the owner of the house; the other he identified positively as Mr Parker.

It was clear now that the Parkers had come to Leigh House to blackmail Protheroe, and when later it was discovered that the dead man's real name was Wendover, and that he had been a lieutenant in the Navy and had been concerned in the blowing up of the first-class cruiser *Merrythought*, in 1910, the case seemed to be rapidly clearing. It was supposed that Parker, cognizant of the part Wendover had played, had tracked him down and demanded hush-money which the other refused to pay. In the course of the quarrel, Wendover drew his revolver, and Parker snatched it from him and shot him, subsequently endeavouring to give it the appearance of suicide.

Parker was committed for trial, reserving his defence. We had attended the police-court proceedings. As we left, Poirot nodded his head.

'It must be so,' he murmured to himself. 'Yes, it must be so. I will delay no longer.'

He went into the post office, and wrote off a note which he despatched by special messenger. I did not see to whom it was addressed. Then we returned to the inn where we had stayed on that memorable weekend.

Poirot was restless, going to and from the window.

'I await a visitor,' he explained. 'It cannot be – surely it cannot be that I am mistaken? No, here she is.'

To my utter astonishment, in another minute Miss Clegg walked into the room. She was less calm than usual, and was breathing hard as though she had been running. I saw the fear in her eyes as she looked at Poirot.

'Sit down, mademoiselle,' he said kindly. 'I guessed rightly, did I not?'

For answer she burst into tears.

'Why did you do it?' asked Poirot gently. 'Why?'

'I loved him so,' she answered. 'I was nursemaid to him when he was a little boy. Oh, be merciful to me!'

'I will do all I can. But you understand that I cannot permit an innocent man to hang – even though he is an unpleasing scoundrel.'

She sat up and said in a low voice: 'Perhaps in the end I could not have, either. Do whatever must be done.'

Then, rising, she hurried from the room.

'Did she shoot him?' I asked utterly bewildered.

Poirot smiled and shook his head.

'He shot himself. Do you remember that he carried his handkerchief in his *right* sleeve? That showed me that he was left-handed. Fearing exposure, after his stormy interview with Mr Parker, he shot himself. In the morning Miss Clegg came to call him as usual and found him lying dead. As she has just told us, she had known him from a little boy upward, and was filled with fury against the Parkers, who had driven him to this shameful death. She regarded them as murderers, and then suddenly she saw a chance of making them suffer for the deed they had inspired. She alone knew that he was left-handed. She changed the pistol to his right hand, closed and bolted the window, dropped the bit of cuff-link she had picked up in one of the downstairs rooms, and went out, locking the door and removing the key.'

'Poirot,' I said, in a burst of enthusiasm, 'you are magnificent. All that from the one little clue of the handkerchief.'

'And the cigarette-smoke. If the window had been closed, and all those cigarettes smoked, the room ought to have been full of stale tobacco. Instead, it was perfectly fresh, so I deduced at once that the window must have been open all night, and only closed in the morning, and that gave me a very interesting line of speculation. I could conceive of no circumstances under which a murderer could want to shut the window. It would be to his advantage to leave it open, and pretend that the murderer had escaped that way, if the theory of suicide did not go down. Of course, the tramp's evidence, when I heard it, confirmed my suspicions. He could never have overheard that conversation unless the window had been open.'

'Splendid!' I said heartily. 'Now, what about some tea?'

'Spoken like a true Englishman,' said Poirot with a sigh. 'I suppose it is not likely that I could obtain here a glass of *sirop*?'

WASPS' NEST

Out of the house came John Harrison and stood a moment on the terrace looking out over the garden. He was a big man with a lean, cadaverous face. His aspect was usually somewhat grim but when, as now, the rugged features softened into a smile, there was something very attractive about him.

John Harrison loved his garden, and it had never looked better than it did on this August evening, summery and languorous. The rambler roses were still beautiful; sweet peas scented the air.

A well-known creaking sound made Harrison turn his head sharply. Who was coming in through the garden gate? In another minute, an expression of utter astonishment came over his face, for the dandified figure coming up the path was the last he expected to see in this part of the world.

'By all that's wonderful,' cried Harrison. 'Monsieur Poirot!'

It was, indeed, the famous Hercule Poirot whose renown as a detective had spread over the whole world.

'Yes,' he said, 'it is. You said to me once: "If you are ever in this part of the world, come and see me." I take you at your word. I arrive.'

'And I'm obliged,' said Harrison heartily. 'Sit down and have a drink.'

With a hospitable hand, he indicated a table on the veranda bearing assorted bottles.

'I thank you,' said Poirot, sinking down into a basket chair. 'You have, I suppose, no *sirop*? No, no. I thought not. A little plain soda water then – no whisky.' And he added in a feeling voice as the other placed the glass beside him: 'Alas, my moustaches are limp. It is this heat!'

'And what brings you into this quiet spot?' asked Harrison as he dropped into another chair. 'Pleasure?'

'No, *mon ami*, business.'

'Business? In this out-of-the-way place?'

Poirot nodded gravely. 'But yes, my friend, all crimes are not committed in crowds, you know?'

The other laughed. 'I suppose that was rather an idiotic remark of mine. But what particular crime are you investigating down here, or is that a thing I mustn't ask?'

'You may ask,' said the detective. 'Indeed, I would prefer that you asked.'

Harrison looked at him curiously. He sensed something a little unusual in the other's manner. 'You are investigating a crime, you say?' he advanced rather hesitatingly. 'A serious crime?'

'A crime of the most serious there is.'

'You mean ...'

'Murder.'

So gravely did Hercule Poirot say that word that Harrison was quite taken aback. The detective was looking straight at him and again there was something so unusual in his glance that Harrison hardly knew how to proceed. At last, he said: 'But I have heard of no murder.'

'No,' said Poirot, 'you would not have heard of it.'

'Who has been murdered?'

'As yet,' said Hercule Poirot, 'nobody.'

'What?'

'That is why I said you would not have heard of it. I am investigating a crime that has not yet taken place.'

'But look here, that is nonsense.'

'Not at all. If one can investigate a murder before it has happened, surely that is very much better than afterwards. One might even – a little idea – prevent it.'

Harrison stared at him. 'You are not serious, Monsieur Poirot.'

'But yes, I am serious.'

'You really believe that a murder is going to be committed? Oh, it's absurd!'

Hercule Poirot finished the first part of the sentence without taking any notice of the exclamation.

'Unless we can manage to prevent it. Yes, *mon ami*, that is what I mean.'

'We?'

'I said we. I shall need your co-operation.'

'Is that why you came down here?'

Again Poirot looked at him, and again an indefinable something made Harrison uneasy.

'I came here, Monsieur Harrison because I – well – like you.'

And then he added in an entirely different voice: 'I see, Monsieur Harrison, that you have a wasps' nest there. You should destroy it.'

The change of subject made Harrison frown in a puzzled way. He followed Poirot's glance and said in a bewildered voice: 'As a matter of fact, I'm going to. Or rather, young Langton is. You remember Claude Langton? He was at that same dinner where I met you. He's coming over this evening to take the nest. Rather fancies himself at the job.'

'Ah,' said Poirot. 'And how is he going to do it?'

'Petrol and the garden syringe. He's bringing his own syringe over; it's a more convenient size than mine.'

'There is another way, is there not?' asked Poirot. 'With cyanide of potassium?'

Harrison looked a little surprised. 'Yes, but that's rather dangerous stuff. Always a risk having it about the place.'

Poirot nodded gravely. 'Yes, it is deadly poison.' He waited a minute and then repeated in a grave voice, 'Deadly poison.'

'Useful if you want to do away with your mother-in-law, eh?' said Harrison with a laugh.

But Hercule Poirot remained grave. 'And you are quite sure, Monsieur Harrison, that it is with petrol that Monsieur Langton is going to destroy your wasps' nest?'

'Quite sure. Why?'

'I wondered. I was at the chemist's in Barchester this afternoon. For one of my purchases I had to sign the poison book. I saw the last entry. It was for cyanide of potassium and it was signed by Claude Langton.'

Harrison stared. 'That's odd,' he said. 'Langton told me the other day that he'd never dream of using the stuff; in fact, he said it oughtn't to be sold for the purpose.'

Poirot looked out over the garden. His voice was very quiet as he asked a question. 'Do you like Langton?'

The other started. The question somehow seemed to find him quite unprepared. 'I – I – well, I mean – of course, I like him. Why shouldn't I?'

'I only wondered,' said Poirot placidly, 'whether you did.'

And as the other did not answer, he went on. 'I also wondered if he liked you?'

'What are you getting at, Monsieur Poirot? There's something in your mind I can't fathom.'

'I am going to be very frank. You are engaged to be married, Monsieur Harrison. I know Miss Molly Deane. She is a very charming, a very beautiful girl. Before she was engaged to you, she was engaged to Claude Langton. She threw him over for you.'

Harrison nodded.

'I do not ask what her reasons were: she may have been justified. But I tell you this, it is not too much to suppose that Langton has not forgotten or forgiven.'

'You're wrong, Monsieur Poirot. I swear you're wrong. Langton's been a sportsman; he's taken things like a man. He's been amazingly decent to me – gone out of his way to be friendly.'

'And that does not strike you as unusual? You use the word "amazingly", but you do not seem to be amazed.'

'What do you mean, M. Poirot?'

'I mean,' said Poirot, and his voice had a new note in it, 'that a man may conceal his hate till the proper time comes.'

'Hate?' Harrison shook his head and laughed.

'The English are very stupid,' said Poirot. 'They think that they can deceive anyone but that no one can deceive them. The sportsman – the good fellow – never will they believe evil of him. And because they are brave, but stupid, sometimes they die when they need not die.'

'You are warning me,' said Harrison in a low voice. 'I see it now – what has puzzled me all along. You are warning me against Claude Langton. You came here today to warn me ...'

Poirot nodded. Harrison sprang up suddenly. 'But *you* are mad, Monsieur Poirot. This is England. Things don't happen like that here. Disappointed suitors don't go about stabbing people in the back and poisoning them. And you're wrong about Langton. That chap wouldn't hurt a fly.'

'The lives of flies are not my concern,' said Poirot placidly. 'And although you say Monsieur Langton would not take the life of one, yet you forget that he is even now preparing to take the lives of several thousand wasps.'

Harrison did not at once reply. The little detective in his turn sprang to his feet. He advanced to his friend and laid a hand on his shoulder. So agitated was he that he almost shook the big man, and, as he did so, he hissed into his ear: 'Rouse yourself, my friend, rouse yourself. And look – look where I am pointing. There on the bank, close by that tree root. See you, the wasps returning home, placid at the end of the day? In a little hour, there will be destruction, and they know it not. There is no one to tell them. They have not, it seems, a Hercule Poirot. I tell you, Monsieur Harrison, I am down here on business. Murder is my business. And it is my business before it has happened as well as afterwards. At what time does Monsieur Langton come to take this wasps' nest?'

'Langton would never ...'

'At what time?'

'At nine o'clock. But I tell you, you're all wrong. Langton would never ...'

'These English!' cried Poirot in a passion. He caught up his hat and stick and moved down the path, pausing to speak over his shoulder. 'I do not stay to argue with you. I should only enrage myself. But you understand, I return at nine o'clock?'

Harrison opened his mouth to speak, but Poirot did not give him the chance. 'I know what you would say: "Langton would never", et cetera. Ah, Langton would never! But all the same I return at nine o'clock. But, yes, it will amuse me – put it like that – it will amuse me to see the taking of a wasps' nest. Another of your English sports!'

He waited for no reply but passed rapidly down the path and out through the door that creaked. Once outside on the road, his pace slackened. His vivacity died down, his face became grave and troubled. Once he drew his watch from his pocket and consulted it. The hands pointed to ten minutes past eight. 'Over three quarters of an hour,' he murmured. 'I wonder if I should have waited.'

His footsteps slackened; he almost seemed on the point of returning. Some vague foreboding seemed to assail him. He shook it off resolutely, however, and continued to walk in the direction of the village. But his face was still troubled, and once or twice he shook his head like a man only partly satisfied.

It was still some minutes off nine when he once more approached the garden door. It was a clear, still evening; hardly a breeze stirred the leaves. There was, perhaps, something a little sinister in the stillness, like the lull before a storm.

Poirot's footsteps quickened ever so slightly. He was suddenly alarmed – and uncertain. He feared he knew not what.

And at that moment the garden door opened and Claude Langton stepped quickly out into the road. He started when he saw Poirot.

'Oh – er – good evening.'

'Good evening, Monsieur Langton. You are early.'

Langton stared at him. 'I don't know what you mean.'

'You have taken the wasps' nest?'

'As a matter of fact, I didn't.'

'Oh,' said Poirot softly. 'So you did not take the wasps' nest. What did you do then?'

'Oh, just sat and yarned a bit with old Harrison. I really must hurry along now, Monsieur Poirot. I'd no idea you were remaining in this part of the world.'

'I had business here, you see.'

'Oh! Well, you'll find Harrison on the terrace. Sorry I can't stop.'

He hurried away. Poirot looked after him. A nervous young fellow, good-looking with a weak mouth!

'So I shall find Harrison on the terrace,' murmured Poirot.

'I wonder.' He went in through the garden door and up the path. Harrison was sitting in a chair by the table. He sat motionless and did not even turn his head as Poirot came up to him.

'Ah! *Mon ami*,' said Poirot. 'You are all right, eh?'

There was a long pause and then Harrison said in a queer, dazed voice, 'What did you say?'

'I said – are you all right?'

'All right? Yes, I'm all right. Why not?'

'You feel no ill effects? That is good.'

'Ill effects? From what?'

'Washing soda.'

Harrison roused himself suddenly. 'Washing soda? What do you mean?'

Poirot made an apologetic gesture. 'I infinitely regret the necessity, but I put some in your pocket.'

'You put some in my pocket? What on earth for?'

Harrison stared at him. Poirot spoke quietly and imperson-ally like a lecturer coming down to the level of a small child.

'You see, one of the advantages, or disadvantages, of being a detective is that it brings you into contact with the criminal classes. And the criminal classes, they can teach you some very interesting and curious things. There was a pickpocket once – I interested myself in him because for once in a way he had not done what they say he has done – and so I get him off. And because he is grateful he pays me in the only way he can think of – which is to show me the tricks of his trade.

'And so it happens that I can pick a man's pocket if I choose without his ever suspecting the fact. I lay one hand on his shoulder, I excite myself, and he feels nothing. But all the same I have managed to transfer what is in his pocket to my pocket and leave washing soda in its place.

'You see,' continued Poirot dreamily, 'if a man wants to get at some poison quickly to put in a glass, unobserved, he positively must keep it in his right-hand coat pocket; there is nowhere else. I knew it would be there.'

He dropped his hand into his pocket and brought out a few

white, lumpy crystals. 'Exceedingly dangerous,' he murmured, 'to carry it like that – loose.'

Calmly and without hurrying himself, he took from another pocket a wide-mouthed bottle. He slipped in the crystals, stepped to the table and filled up the bottle with plain water. Then carefully corking it, he shook it until all the crystals were dissolved. Harrison watched him as though fascinated.

Satisfied with his solution, Poirot stepped across to the nest. He uncorked the bottle, turned his head aside, and poured the solution into the wasps' nest, then stood back a pace or two watching.

Some wasps that were returning alighted, quivered a little and then lay still. Other wasps crawled out of the hole only to die. Poirot watched for a minute or two and then nodded his head and came back to the veranda.

'A quick death,' he said. 'A very quick death.'

Harrison found his voice. 'How much do you know?'

Poirot looked straight ahead. 'As I told you, I saw Claude Langton's name in the book. What I did not tell you was that almost immediately afterwards, I happened to meet him. He told me he had been buying cyanide of potassium at your request – to take a wasps' nest. That struck me as a little odd, my friend, because I remember that at that dinner of which you spoke, you held forth on the superior merits of petrol and denounced the buying of cyanide as dangerous and unnecessary.'

'Go on.'

'I knew something else. I had seen Claude Langton and Molly Deane together when they thought no one saw them. I do not know what lovers' quarrel it was that originally parted them and drove her into your arms, but I realized that misunderstandings were over and that Miss Deane was drifting back to her love.'

'Go on.'

'I knew something more, my friend. I was in Harley Street the other day, and I saw you come out of a certain doctor's house. I know the doctor and for what disease one consults him, and I read the expression on your face. I have seen it only once or twice in my lifetime, but it is not easily mistaken. It was the face of a man under sentence of death. I am right, am I not?'

'Quite right. He gave me two months.'

'You did not see me, my friend, for you had other things to think about. I saw something else on your face – the thing that I told you this afternoon men try to conceal. I saw hate there, my friend. You did not trouble to conceal it, because you thought there were none to observe.'

'Go on,' said Harrison.

'There is not much more to say. I came down here, saw Langton's name by accident in the poison book as I tell you, met him, and came here to you. I laid traps for you. You denied having asked Langton to get cyanide, or rather you expressed surprise at his having done so. You were taken aback at first at my appearance, but presently you saw how well it would fit in and you encouraged my suspicions. I knew from Langton himself that he was coming at half past eight. You told me nine o'clock, thinking I should come and find everything over. And so I knew everything.'

'Why did you come?' cried Harrison. 'If only you hadn't come!'

Poirot drew himself up. 'I told you,' he said, 'murder is my business.'

'Murder? Suicide, you mean.'

'No.' Poirot's voice rang out sharply and clearly. 'I mean murder. Your death was to be quick and easy, but the death you planned for Langton was the worst death any man can die. He bought the poison; he comes to see you, and he is alone with you. You die suddenly, and the cyanide is found in your glass, and Claude Langton hangs. That was your plan.'

Again Harrison moaned.

'Why did you come? Why did you come?'

'I have told you, but there is another reason. I liked you. Listen, *mon ami*, you are a dying man; you have lost the girl you loved, but there is one thing that you are not; you are not a murderer. Tell me now: are you glad or sorry that I came?'

There was a moment's pause and Harrison drew himself up. There was a new dignity in his face – the look of a man who has

92

conquered his own baser self. He stretched out his hand across the table.

'Thank goodness you came,' he cried. 'Oh, thank goodness you came.'

ALSO BY AGATHA CHRISTIE

And Then
There Were None

Ten strangers find themselves trapped in a lonely
island mansion off the Devon coast. Ten strangers
who have nothing in common – except that each one
guards a deadly secret.

Then the murderer strikes – and there are only nine.
Then eight. Then seven.
Then six. Then five.
Then four. Then three . . .

ISBN 0 00 616540 0

Sad Cypress

Young and beautiful . . .

Elinor Carlisle stands in the dock, accused of murdering Mary Gerrard. The court is packed with people, watching and wondering, all convinced of her guilt. The evidence against her is unassailable. But Hercule Poirot is not at all convinced . . .

'Poirot solves another tough, exciting case'
Daily Mail

'Agatha Christie has done it again, which is all you need to know!'
Observer

ISBN 0 00 616720 9